EX LIBRIS

ALSO BY RUTH RENDELL

Ruth Rendell

Dark Corners

HUTCHINSON
LONDON

1 3 5 7 9 10 8 6 4 2

Hutchinson
20 Vauxhall Bridge Road
London sw1v 2sa

Hutchinson is part of the Penguin Random House group of companies
whose addresses can be found at global.penguinrandomhouse.com

First published in Great Britain in 2015 by
Hutchinson

www.randomhouse.co.uk

A CIP catalogue record for this book
is available from the British Library.

isbn 9780091959241 (hardback)
isbn 9780091959258 (trade paperback)

Penguin Random House is committed to a sustainable future for our business,
our readers and our planet. This book is made from Forest Stewardship Council® certified paper.

Typeset in Fairfield LT Std by Palimpsest Book Production Limited, Falkirk, Stirlingshire

Printed and bound by Clays Ltd, St Ives plc

AN INTERVIEW WITH
RUTH RENDELL

'But why the fascination with psychopaths? . . .

"Well," Rendell says in her precise voice, "I do empathise with people who are driven by dreadful impulses. I think to be driven to want to kill must be such a terrible burden. I try, and I think I succeed, in making my readers feel pity for my psychopaths, because *I* do."'

Sunday Telegraph magazine, 10 April 2005

CHAPTER ONE

F or many years Wilfred Martin collected samples of alternative medicines, homeopathic remedies and herbal pills. Most of them he never used, never even tried because he was afraid of them, but he kept the lot in a cupboard in a bathroom in his house in Falcon Mews, Maida Vale, and when he died they went, along with the house and its contents, to his son Carl.

Carl's mother recommended throwing it all out. It was junk, harmless at best, possibly dangerous, all those bottles and jars and sachets just taking up room. But Carl didn't throw it out because he couldn't be bothered. He had other things to do. If he had known how it, or one particular item among all the rest, would change his life, transform it, ruin it, he would have emptied the lot into a plastic bag, carried the bag down the road and dumped it in the big rubbish bin.

C arl had taken over the former family home in Falcon Mews at the beginning of the year, his mother having moved to Camden when his parents divorced. For a while he thought no more about the contents of his bathroom cupboard. He was occupied with his girlfriend Nicola, his novel *Death's Door*, which had just been published, and with letting the top floor of his house. He had no need of those two rooms plus kitchen and bathroom, and great need of the rent. Excited though he was about the publication of his first book, he was not so naïve at twenty-three as to suppose he could live by writing alone. Rents in central London had reached a peak, and Falcon Mews, a crescent looping out of Sutherland Avenue to Castellain Road in Maida Vale, was highly desirable and much sought-after. So he placed an advertisement in the *Paddington Express* offering accommodation, and next morning twenty prospective tenants presented themselves on his doorstep. Why he chose the first applicant, Dermot McKinnon, he never knew. Perhaps it was because he didn't want to interview dozens of people. It was a decision he was bitterly to regret.

But not at the beginning. The only drawback Dermot seemed to have was his appearance – his uneven yellow teeth, for instance, his extreme thinness and round shoulders. But you don't decide against a tenant because his looks are unprepossessing, Carl told himself, and no doubt the man could pay the rent. Dermot had a job at the Sutherland Pet Clinic in the next street and produced a reference from the chief veterinarian there. Carl asked him to pay each month's rent at the end of the previous month, and perhaps the first mistake he made was to request that it be paid not by transfer into his bank account, but in notes or a cheque in an envelope left at Carl's door. Carl realised that these days this was unusual, but he wanted to see the rent come in, take it in his hand. Dermot put up no objection.

Carl had already begun work on a second novel, having been encouraged by his agent Susanna Griggs to get on with it. He didn't expect an advance payment until he had finished it and Susanna and his editor had read and accepted it. There was no payment promised on paperback publication of *Death's Door*, as no one expected it to go into paperback. Still, what with being both a published author with good prospects and a landlord receiving rent, Carl felt rich.

Dermot had to enter Carl's house by the front door and go up two flights of stairs to get to his flat, but he made no noise and, as he put it, kept himself to himself. Carl had already noticed his tenant was a master of the cliché. And for a while everything seemed fine, the rent paid promptly in twenty-pound notes in an envelope on the last day of the month.

All the houses in Falcon Mews were rather small, all different in shape and colour, and all joined together in long rows facing each other. The road surface was cobbled except for where the two ends of the mews met Sutherland Avenue and where the residents could park their cars. The house Carl had inherited was painted ochre, with white window frames and white window boxes. It had a small, very overgrown back garden with a wooden shack at the end full of broken tools and a defunct lawnmower.

As for the alternative medicine, Carl took a couple of doses of something called benzoic acid when he had a cold. It claimed to suppress phlegm and coughs, but it had no effect. Apart from that, he had never looked inside the cupboard where all the bottles and jars lived.

Dermot McKinnon set off for the Sutherland Pet Clinic at twenty to nine each morning, returning to his flat at five thirty. On Sundays he went to church. If Dermot hadn't told him, Carl would never have guessed that he was a church-goer, attending one of the several churches in the neighbourhood, St Saviour's in Warwick Avenue, for instance, or St Mary's, Paddington Green.

They encountered each other in the mews on a Sunday morning and Dermot said, 'Just off to morning service.'

'Really?'

'I'm a regular attender,' said Dermot, adding, 'The better the day, the better the deed.'

Carl was on his way to have a coffee with his friend Stacey Warren. They had met at school, then gone to university together, where Carl had read philosophy and Stacey had taken a drama course. It was while she was still at university that her parents had been killed in a car crash and Stacey inherited quite a lot of money, enough to buy herself a flat in Primrose Hill. Stacey wanted to act, and because of her beautiful face and slender figure was given a significant part in a TV sitcom called *Station Road*. Her face became known to the public overnight, while her slenderness was lost in a few months.

'I've put on a stone,' she said to Carl across the table in their local Café Rouge. 'What am I going to do?' Other customers were giving her not very surreptitious glances. 'They all know who I am. They're all thinking I'm getting fat. What's going to happen to me?'

Carl, who was very thin, had no idea how much he weighed and didn't care. 'You'll have to go on a diet, I suppose.'

'David and I have split up. I'm finding that very hard to take. Have I got to starve myself too?'

'I don't know anything about diets, Stacey. You don't need to starve, do you?'

'I'd rather take one of those magic diet pills that get advertised online. D'you know anything about them?'

'Why would I?' said Carl. 'Not my kind of thing.'

The waitress brought the two chocolate brownies and the slice of carrot cake Stacey had ordered. Carl said nothing.

'I didn't have any breakfast,' she said.

Carl just nodded.

On his way home, still thinking about Stacey and her problem, he passed the bookshop kept by his friend Will Finsford. It was the one remaining privately run bookshop for miles around, and Will had confided that he lay awake at night worrying about having to close, especially as the organic shop down the road had not only gone out of business but had had the bailiffs in.

Carl saw him rearranging the display of best-sellers in the window and went in.

'D'you have any books on losing weight, Will?'

5

Will looked him up and down. 'You already look like you're wasting away.'

'Not for me. For a girl I know.'

'Not the beautiful Nicola, I hope?' said Will.

'No, for someone else. A friend who's got fat. That's a word I'm not supposed to say, isn't it?'

'You're safe with me. Have a look along the shelves, health section.'

Carl found nothing he thought would be suitable. 'Come over one evening, why don't you?' he said. 'Bring Corinne. The beautiful Nicola would love to see you. We'll ring you.'

Will said he would and went back to his window arrangement.

Walking home, Carl realised it wasn't really a book he wanted. Stacey had mentioned pills. He wondered if there were any slimming medications among his father's stash of pills and potions, as he had come to think of them. Wilfred Martin had always been thin so was unlikely to have used that sort of thing, but some drugs claimed to serve a double purpose, improving the skin, for instance, or curing indigestion.

Carl thought of his father, a rather taciturn, quirky man. He was sorry Wilfred was gone, but they had never had much in common. He regretted that his father had not lived to see *Death's Door* published. But he had left Carl the house, with its income potential. Had that been his way of offering his blessing on his son's chosen career? Carl hoped so.

The house was silent when he got in, but it usually

6

was whether Dermot was at home or not. He was a good tenant. Carl went upstairs and saw that the bathroom door was open. Dermot had his own bathroom in his flat on the top floor, so had no reason to use this one. Probably he'd forgotten to close the door himself, Carl thought, as he went into the bathroom, shutting the door behind him.

Wilfred's pills and potions were in a cupboard divided into five sections on the left-hand side of the washbasin. Only the topmost section was for Carl's current use; he didn't need much space, as his toothbrush and toothpaste and roll-on deodorant were on the shelf above the basin. Surveying the collection of bottles and phials and jars and packages, tubes and cans and blister packs, he asked himself why he had kept all this stuff. Surely not for its sentimental value. He had loved his father, but he had never felt like that about him. On the contrary, he regarded the pills and potions as mostly quack remedies, rubbish really, and quite useless. A lot of the products, he saw, taking small jars out at random, claimed to treat heart problems and safeguard against heart failure, yet his father had had two heart attacks and died after the second one.

No, there was nothing here that would encourage weight loss, Carl told himself. Best throw it all out, make a clean sweep. But what was that in a large plastic zip-up bag in the second section from the top? Yellow capsules, a great many of them, labelled DNP. *The foolproof way to avoid weight gain!* promised the label. Behind the bag of capsules was a box full of sachets also containing DNP but in powder-to-liquid form.

Taking the plastic bag out, he noted that, further down, the label advised using with care, and not to exceed the stated dose, etc. etc. The usual small print. But even paracetamol containers said that. He left the bag of capsules where it was and went downstairs to look up DNP on the computer. But before he got there, the front doorbell rang and he remembered that Nicola – beautiful, clever, sweet Nicola – was coming to spend the rest of the day and the night with him. He went to let her in, telling himself he must give her a key. He wanted her as a more permanent part of his life. With Nicola, his new novel and a reliable tenant, life was good.

For the time being, he forgot all about the slimming pills.

CHAPTER TWO

At first, being a landlord seemed trouble-free. Dermot paid his rent on the appointed day with the minimum of fuss. That is, he did for the first two months. The thirty-first of March was a Monday, and at 8.30 Carl was, as usual, eating his breakfast when he heard Dermot's footsteps on the stairs. Generally they would be followed by a tap at the door, but this time they were not. The front door closed, and Carl, getting up to look out of the window, saw Dermot walking down the mews towards Sutherland Avenue. Maybe the rent would come later today, he thought.

Carl seldom saw a newspaper except for selected bits online, but he bought a couple of papers on 1 April to see if he could spot the jokes. The best one he had ever heard of – it was published before he was born – was the story that the arms of the Venus de Milo had been found washed up on some Mediterranean beach. Still, today's made him laugh, and by the time he got to his mother's flat, he had forgotten all about the missing rent. It was her birthday as well as April Fool's Day, and Carl

9

was invited to a celebration lunch along with a cousin and two close friends. His mother asked him if she should have invited his girlfriend, and he said Nicola would still be at work in the Department of Health in Whitehall. It was a lovely sunny day and he walked halfway home before getting on the 46 bus.

But there was still the matter of the late rent. There was no sign of an envelope from Dermot. Carl woke up very early the next morning worrying. He disliked the idea of confronting Dermot; he found he had broken into a sweat just thinking about it. He was drinking a mug of very strong coffee when he heard Dermot's footsteps. If the front door opened, he told himself, he would make himself go out and ask for the money. Instead, Dermot tapped on the kitchen door and handed over an envelope. Smiling and showing his horrible yellowish teeth he said, 'Did you think I was playing an April Fool's joke?'

'What? No, no, of course not.'

'Just a mistake,' said Dermot. 'He who makes no mistakes makes nothing. See you later.'

Carl felt great relief, but just to make sure, he counted the notes. And there it was, as it should be: twelve hundred pounds. Not nearly enough, his mother had said, considering today's prices, but it seemed a lot to Carl.

He filled a bowl with muesli because he was suddenly hungry, but the milk had gone sour so he had to throw the contents of the bowl away. Apart from the milk, though, things were going well and it was a good time to get back to work on his new novel, a more serious venture than his first. Carl looked at the notes he had made about Highgate Cemetery, the research he was doing for his first four chapters. Perhaps he should have made another visit to the cemetery yesterday, but he thought he had enough material to write his first chapter. The only interruption was a phone call from Stacey. It surprised him the way friends unloaded their trivial (it seemed to him) concerns.

'I'm so sorry, Carl.' She seemed to think the simple apology was enough to permit a long misery moan about her weight.

'I'm working, Stacey,' he said.

'Oh, writing, you mean?'

He sighed. People always said that, as if writing were quick and easy. Should he mention the DNP? No, it wouldn't shut her up. On the contrary, it would fetch her round here, and as much as he liked her, he needed to work. Instead he listened, making sympathetic noises, until he told the white lie those who work from home sometimes have to employ.

'Got to go, Stacey. There's someone at the door.'

He still couldn't write. It was absurd and something to feel a little ashamed of, suddenly to be happy, to be carefree, because he'd received a packet with twelve hundred pounds in it. Money that was rightly his, that was owed to him. Now he came to think of it, the rent money was his sole secure income. He couldn't count on more book money for a long time. The rent brought him relief and happiness.

He definitely wouldn't be able to write today. The sun

was shining and he would go out, walk up to the big green space that was Paddington Recreation Ground, lie on the grass in the sun and look up through the branches at the blue sky.

CHAPTER THREE

I t wasn't April Fool's Day or even May Day but 2 May when the next rent payment arrived.

Carl wasn't as nervous as he had been the previous month. Nicola had spent the night with him, but he had said nothing to her about the rent being late in April. After all, it had come and all had been well. She had gone to work on 2 May before Dermot left the house, so she wasn't there to see Carl listening for his tenant's footfalls on the stair or to see his surprise when the front door closed without Dermot's tap on the kitchen door. Perhaps the rent would come later in the day, and this was in fact what happened.

They encountered each other in the hallway, Carl leaving the house to do some food shopping and Dermot coming in at five thirty from the pet clinic.

'I've got something for you,' said Dermot, handing over an envelope.

Carl thought it strange that Dermot should have carried that envelope containing twelve hundred pounds about with him all day, but still, it wasn't important: he had got his money. He wouldn't have to break into his very meagre and dwindling savings in order to go on a week's holiday with Nicola. They would only be going to Cornwall, not abroad anywhere, but he was looking forward to their stay in Fowey.

Stacey had phoned again in some despair before they left, but on his mobile this time. He told her he was going away but that she must come over to see him when he got back. They'd go out to eat and he would see what he could do to help with her weight problem. Why had he said that? It must have been the DNP that had come into his mind. He dismissed it. He couldn't help anyone lose weight.

He and Nicola went to Fowey with the couple who had introduced them, and who were still special friends partly for that reason. They had a good time, and by the time they got back to Paddington station, Carl had asked Nicola to come to Falcon Mews. 'I mean to live with me,' he said. 'Permanently.' He felt good about Nicola. They cared about the same things – books, music, the outdoors. She loved that he was a writer. He loved her.

'I'll have to go back to my flat and tell my flatmates, but then I will. I want to. I'd been going to ask you, but . . . well, I must be sort of old-fashioned. I thought it wouldn't be right for me to ask and not you. Me being a woman, I mean.'

She moved in three days later.

*

14

The day before Nicola moved in, Stacey came round. She and Carl planned to go out to eat at a nearby restaurant. Before that, Stacey used his bathroom to renew her make-up. Perhaps because of her acting and her modelling, she made up very heavily, especially around her eyes.

After a few minutes, Carl went upstairs to fetch himself an antihistamine pill for his hay fever. He left the bathroom door ajar. Stacey followed him in. She was one of those people who, when someone told her of a mild illness or problem, always claimed to suffer from the same complaint. 'Funny you should say that, because I've got hay fever too.' He opened the cabinet and found the antihistamines on the top shelf. Stacey was standing behind him, telling him about her symptoms and peering over his shoulder.

'Where did all this stuff come from?' she asked. 'Do you use it?'

'It was my dad's. I sort of inherited it – you know, when I got the house and the furniture and everything.'

He reached into the cabinet and brought out the package with the yellow capsules. 'This is supposed to make you lose weight. I expect he got it online.'

'Did your dad use it?'

'He can't have. He was so thin he was practically a skeleton.'

She took the package from his hand and looked at it. 'DNP,' she said. 'Dinitrophenol. One hundred capsules.' Then she read the instructions and looked at the price marked on the package. One hundred pounds.

Carl took the bag from her and replaced it on the shelf, but not at the back.

'I could order some online,' she said. 'But – well, you've already got these. Would you sell me fifty?'

Sell them? He knew he should just give them to her, but the hotel he and Nicola had stayed in in Fowey had been pricey, the restaurants they had visited in various other Cornish resorts as expensive as London – the kind they never went to in London – and the holiday, though the costs had been shared with Nicola, far more expensive than he had expected. Fifty pounds for these pills wasn't all that much, but it would be a help. And Stacey could afford it; well, she certainly could if she lost that weight and kept her sitcom job.

'OK,' he said, as he counted fifty out into a tooth mug and handed her the packet with the fifty remaining in it.

He went downstairs, realising as he did so that Dermot was closing the front door on his way out. Could he have heard his conversation with Stacey as he came down the stairs? Perhaps. But what did it matter if he had?

By now Stacey had finished her make-up and joined him. They were going up the road to Raoul's in Clifton Road. Outside on the pavement she handed over the fifty pounds.

He forgot about the transaction, not least because Nicola had moved in and he wondered why they had waited so long; it had been two years since Jonathan

16

had first introduced them. But his novel wasn't going well and he had reached a stage in which he struggled to produce two or three paragraphs a day. Nicola asked about it, and he always said everything was fine. He had no idea why this writer's block had arisen.

May was a fine warm month in London, and because staring at his computer was useless and unprofitable, Carl had taken to going out in the late morning while Nicola was at work and picking up a copy of the *Evening Standard*. He chose the *Standard* rather than any other daily paper because it was free.

He stared at today's front page. There, in full colour, was a three-column photograph of Stacey. She looked beautiful, not smiling, but in a soulful pose, her long, thick blonde hair draped about her shoulders in a theatrical head shot. Described as twenty-four years old, with her face familiar from her starring role in *Station Road*, she had been found dead in her Primrose Hill flat by a friend who had a key. Police said foul play was not suspected.

It couldn't be – but it must be. Carl broke into a sweat. The phone was ringing as he let himself into the house. It was his mother, Una.

'Oh darling, have you seen the news about poor Stacey?'

'It's in the *Standard*.'

'She was so lovely before she put on all that weight. There was a time when I thought you might marry her.'

His mother belonged to a generation where women always thought in terms of marriage. Useless to tell her, though he often had, that even girls seldom thought about marriage any more. The subject only came up when they became pregnant, and often not even then.

'Well, I can't marry her now, can I? She's dead.'

'Oh *darling.*'

'We were friends,' he said. 'That's all.'

His mother's words hardly penetrated as he thought about Stacey. He couldn't believe she was dead. She had eaten for comfort, he supposed. Her addiction to food had been the opposite of anorexia. When there was food around, especially butter and cheese and ham and fruit cake and anything in a rich sauce, she would declare that she mustn't touch the stuff, she shouldn't dream of touching it, but she couldn't resist. And as he watched her grow larger, visibly it seemed, increasing each time he saw her, he stopped seeing her, only going over to her flat in Pinetree Court, Primrose Hill, when she begged him not to desert her, please, please to come. And then it seemed to him that she stuffed down food in front of him to annoy. Of course, that couldn't have been her motive, but it seemed like it, especially when mayonnaise dribbled down her chin, fragments of carrot cake or macaroons stuck all over a close-fitting angora sweater, and her once beautiful breasts were transformed into vast mounds of sticky cake crumbs.

They had never been lovers but they had been best friends. Now she was gone.

'A man and a woman can't be friends,' said his mother. 'I wonder if that's what was wrong, that she ate for comfort.'

'You mean if I'd married her she'd have stopped eating?'

'Don't be silly, Carl.'

He imagined himself married to Stacey and walking along Sutherland Avenue beside her, an increasingly ridiculous sight. He was very thin, which had nothing to do with what he ate or didn't eat and everything to do with his thin mother and thin father.

He sat down in front of the computer and touched the tiny switch with its blue light. The screen showed him its usual picture, a green hill and a purple mountain behind it. Dermot had once come in just after he had switched it on and started singing some hymn about a green hill far away without a city wall. Now every time Carl saw the screen he thought about that stupid hymn and sometimes even began humming it. He had meant to move the mouse on to *Sacred Spirits*.doc and try to get back into his novel, but instead he went to the internet, telling himself he had never checked on those yellow capsules he had sold Stacey. The little arrow hovered over Google. He typed in the letters DNP, but went no further. He was afraid.

Shutting his eyes – he didn't want to know, not yet, maybe never – he shifted the cursor to exit.

CHAPTER FOUR

Four days before Carl read the story of Stacey's death, Lizzie Milsom entered Stacey's flat. It was very imprudent to leave the keys to one's home outside the property, and quite difficult to do so when the property was a flat. Still, it was something Stacey Warren did and a good many of her friends knew about it.

There were four flats in Pinetree Court, all with different-coloured front doors. The door to the ground-floor flat was blue, while those to the first- and second-floor flats were yellow and green respectively. A staircase went down to the basement flat, where Stacey had told Lizzie the front door was red. Stacey lived on the first floor; she secreted her two keys on a single ring inside the cupboard underneath the flight of steps that led up to the front door. The cupboard, which had no lock, held the four tenants' waste bins, and there was a loose brick in the floor. Beneath the loose brick, in the hollow space, were Stacey's spare keys.

Because Stacey had told her she would be out that

morning, Lizzie Milsom lifted up the loose brick and helped herself to the keys. She then went into the entrance hall, and went up the stairs to the first floor. Once outside Stacey's flat, she stood still and listened. Silence. All the occupants would be out at work. What she intended to do was find some small object of no great value, an item such as a piece of pottery or a paperweight or a ballpoint pen – the kind of thing a friend might give you for a Christmas present – and take it away with her, having first substituted another valueless object in its place. The latter she had brought with her: a black and white plastic napkin ring. Doing this – and she often did it – gave her a sense of power. People thought their lives were private and safe, but they were not.

She inserted the key in Stacey's yellow front door and let herself in.

Lizzie wasn't beautiful, but she was the kind of girl people called attractive without specifying who they were attractive to. She had lovely blonde hair, thick and long, large innocent brown eyes and pretty hands with nails she kept nice with different-coloured varnish that was never allowed to chip. Her figure was good. She would have liked to dress well but couldn't afford it.

She and Stacey had known each other for years. Their parents' homes had been so near each other that they had walked together to their Brondesbury school, which was just down the road. This wasn't the first time Lizzie had been in Stacey's flat, but it was the first illicit visit. She searched through the living areas, looking for some trinket or useless article, and after a while decided on a small diary, unused and three years out of date but with Stacey's name printed inside the front cover. The napkin ring was substituted and the diary went into Lizzie's bag.

The rooms in Stacey's flat were large. That is, the living room was large and Lizzie assumed the bedroom was too. She devoted half an hour or so to exploring and searching through cupboards and drawers. She had no intention of taking anything else, and what she had taken she would bring back. But she was more inquisitive than most people, and once in a place that wasn't hers was consumed with curiosity. She was also a consummate liar. In the unlikely event of someone entering the place she was exploring, she was always ready with the excuse – she called it a reason – that the owner had asked her to check that she or he had turned off the gas or not left the iron on.

She passed an interesting twenty minutes investigating Stacey's desk drawers, where she found a wad of twenty-pound notes, a bunch of leaflets advertising weight-loss remedies, an unpaid electricity bill and an envelope containing photographs of a naked Stacey taken in the days before she got fat. Lizzie told herself she wasn't a thief and helped herself to only two twenty-pound notes while anyone without principles would have taken the lot. She proceeded to the kitchen, found a half-full bottle of Campari in the fridge, which was otherwise empty of food and drink, and took a swig from it. It made her choke and she wondered what it could have been diluted with. Stacey had a lovely big bathroom, large enough to accommodate an elliptical cross-trainer and a rowing machine. 'She doesn't get much use out of them,' said Lizzie aloud.

She nearly gave the bedroom a miss. She wasn't interested in sorting through Stacey's underwear or trying out her moisturiser. But the Campari had gone to her head and she thought a lie-down might be a good idea. She opened the bedroom door and stopped short. Stacey, in a lacy nightdress and velvet dressing gown, lay on her back on the floor beside her emperor-size bed. A small plastic packet, empty of whatever it had contained, was beside her, and a glass of what was possibly water. Pale yellow capsules were scattered across the pale yellow carpet.

Lizzie knew Stacey was dead, though she couldn't have said how she knew. She didn't scream. Privately she believed that women who screamed when they saw or found a dead body only did it for effect. They could easily have controlled themselves. She made no noise at all.

She knelt down on the floor and felt for Stacey's pulse. But she didn't need that; she only needed the coldness of the skin on her face and the icy dampness of her hands to know that Stacey had been there for a long time, probably since the evening before. She also knew that she had to call the police, or maybe an ambulance, and that now Stacey was dead she really needed no explanation for being in the flat. It would only be a tiny bit awkward. She tapped out 999 on her mobile, and the speed with which it was answered amazed her.

'Police,' she said when presented with options. 'I've just found my best friend dead.'

Stacey wasn't her best friend, but a small lie was necessary. She would have felt cheated if she had told anything in the region of the truth. Saying she had come into the flat with her own set of keys, keys that Stacey had given her, was only a way of supporting the best-friend statement. She mustn't overdo it.

The operator asked her if she would stay in the flat until the police arrived, and she said of course. She sat down, because in spite of her bravado, she felt quite shocked and afraid that she might fall if she stayed standing up. While she waited for the policeman and perhaps others to come, she replaced the diary in the living room and took back her napkin ring. Best do that – suppose they found her DNA on it?

Alone with her thoughts and feeling stronger, Lizzie sat in an armchair in the living room and wondered what would happen to the flat. It had been Stacey's own, free of mortgage, bought with an inheritance from her parents. Stacey had been proud of her financial independence, certain she could carry on with her acting, with big parts in TV serials, once she had lost weight. Her parents had died in a car crash on the M25 when Stacey was at university. She had been staying with her aunt Yvonne Weatherspoon and her aunt's children when the accident happened, and remained with them throughout her time at university. Lizzie wondered if she should phone Yvonne to tell her about Stacey's death, but thought better (or worse) of it. Let the police do that. She didn't have her number, and although she knew Stacey's aunt slightly, she had never got on with her.

In contrast to Stacey, Lizzie lived in a rented bedsit in Iverson Road, Kilburn. The rent was very high for what it was and the place was small, damp and in dire need of redecoration. She thought about it while she sat in Stacey's flat, and thought too how little she wanted to return to it. Her job as a teaching assistant at a private school paid very badly, although it had its advantages. To be able to walk to work was one of them, and a free lunch was another. She wasn't supposed to have a free lunch, or indeed any lunch at school at all, but there was no one to notice her eating from one or more of the many untouched plates she removed from the children's cafeteria. She also ate an evening meal at her parents' once a week, not because she wanted to, but bearing in mind – never for a moment forgetting – that her father paid half her rent. Well, her father *and* her mother, her mother told her she should say, though Lizzie couldn't see why, as her mother didn't work, or wasn't, as she preferred to put it, a wage-earner. A breadwinner, said her father, who had been, until he retired, quite well-off.

Lizzie was thinking rather wistfully of the shepherd's pie and queen of puddings her mother would serve up tonight, when the doorbell rang.

The police had arrived.

CHAPTER FIVE

Carl had never attended an inquest and had no intention of going to this one. That it would happen, and quite soon, loomed very large in his consciousness. He thought about it all the time, though unwillingly, because he would prefer to forget it and dismiss the whole Stacey business from his mind. If he only knew when it was, he could go away somewhere, perhaps to Brighton, or to Broadstairs, where he had once spent a week with a girlfriend. But leaving town wouldn't help him avoid seeing a paper or watching the TV news. Besides, like everything else in his life, he couldn't afford another trip.

Dermot settled the matter for him. He tapped on the living room door on 1 June, the day after rent-payment day, handed over his money (a cheque this time) in the envelope, and said he was on his way to 'the Stacey Warren inquest'. He expected he'd see Carl there, he said.

Carl thought quickly. His nerves wouldn't stand the idea of Dermot hearing all the evidence, even taking notes, and then coming back here and telling him in detail what had happened. He wanted to ask why Dermot was going. He had hardly known Stacey, having met her only once. Carl wanted to tell him that Stacey and her death weren't his business; she had been *his* friend, not Dermot's. But he had no reason to be rude to Dermot, especially as the month's rent had come on time.

'You mustn't think,' Dermot said after Carl had told him he wouldn't be going, 'that I'm taking time off work for this. It happens to coincide with my midday break.' He smiled, showing the yellowish teeth. 'A piece of luck.'

Halfway down the path, he turned, said, 'I'll look in on the way back, tell you what happened.'

He returned several hours later, and seemed to have plenty of time to spare, readily accepting the tea Carl felt constrained to offer. He settled down on the sofa Carl thought of as 'Dad's sofa' with his tea and a Bourbon biscuit, and described the evidence of the doctor and the biochemist in detail.

Dinitrophenol capsules had been lying all over Stacey's bedroom floor, and the same substance was partially digested in her stomach and intestines. The doctor was unable to say if the dose she had recently swallowed was her first or the latest of many. Dinitrophenol – or DNP, as it was called, Dermot said – was known to bring about weight loss, but only if the dose was great enough. A heavy dose or series of doses raised the body temperature far above the danger level and increased the heart rate. Its side effects might be skin lesions, cataracts, damage to the heart and – here he paused – death. The coroner asked a police officer who had been present at the medical examination where this substance could be obtained, and was told it could be bought on the internet.

'The coroner asked this police officer if it wasn't against the law,' said Dermot, 'but he said it wasn't and then he added, "Not yet." Meaning it would be one day, I suppose.'

Carl thought he shouldn't ask but he had to know. 'Did the coroner say anything about where Stacey got this batch of pills?'

Dermot gave him a penetrating look. 'I said: apparently it's obtainable on the internet. All right if I have another biccy?'

Carl pushed the plate in his direction.

'The coroner called Stacey "this poor young woman". He looked quite sad. He said her death should be a warning to all women who were unwise and foolish enough to put the slenderness of their figures before their health.'

'I suppose the verdict was accidental death.'

'That's right,' Dermot said. 'My goodness, look at the time. I must be off. See you later.'

So the coroner had assumed Stacey had bought the pills online. Everyone would assume that. While he was disappointed to have his fears about the DNP confirmed, Carl felt relieved that buying or taking the drug was not against the law, and that therefore, in selling Stacey fifty capsules of it, he had done nothing illegal.

*

Nicola was due home at about six. She used the tube: Westminster to Baker Street, then changed on to the Bakerloo line for Maida Vale. Dermot walked from the veterinary practice in Sutherland Avenue, and this evening he arrived before she did. He was in Carl's living room, and the door was open so there was no avoiding him. He was carrying a large carrot cake in a box.

'Eating all Carl's biscuits the way I did this afternoon, I thought I owed you this.'

'Oh, well, thanks.'

'I'll just have a tiny piece and then I'll leave you in peace. Sorry, didn't mean to make a pun.' Dermot cut himself a generous slice. Addressing Nicola as Miss Townsend, he said he supposed she wouldn't approve of biscuits and rich cake.

She looked doubtfully at him. 'Why not?'

'Well, working at the Department of Health like you do.'

How did he know where she worked? she wondered. Strange. She smiled her 'beautiful Nicola' smile, with a radiant brightness that illuminated the whole of her pretty face. Fortunately Dermot McKinnon could not see beneath the smile to what she was really thinking.

Carl and Dermot were in a café in the Edgware Road, seated at a table covered in animal-print plastic. Dermot had ordered two cappuccinos without asking Carl what he wanted. Carl didn't protest. He was wondering what Dermot's motive in following him in here might be. Silence fell, broken by Dermot asking, while running his fingers across the leopards' spots, if Carl had read in the papers that visitors to zoos shouldn't wear animal-skin prints because they caused excitement inside the cages. Carl hadn't read about it and wasn't interested. The cappuccino, which he had never tasted before, was rich and thick and not much like coffee.

'If I remember rightly,' said Dermot, 'there was some of that DNP stuff that Stacey Warren took among your dad's medicaments.'

An odd word, Carl thought. Medicaments. 'Was there?' he said.

'Perhaps you didn't know what it was?'

'I didn't,' said Carl. He wanted to tell Dermot that he had some nerve, snooping about.

'If you've still got it, you ought to throw it away, you know. I expect there'll be a big story in the papers tomorrow. I expect it will be all about how people shouldn't use DNP and how it ought to be banned. I mean, the law ought to be changed, with a heavy penalty for anyone who gives it to – well, to someone else.'

There was indeed a big story the next day. It was on the front page of the *Daily Mail*, with a glamour photo of Stacey and a picture underneath of yellow capsules in a glass jar labelled DNP.

Carl saw the *Mail* on the rack outside a newsagent. He initially wasn't going to buy it and walked away, then went back when he feared perhaps he might regret not doing so. He read the story as he walked along. One of the things it said was that as a result of Stacey's death from 'DNP poisoning', dinitrophenol would soon be banned, which could happen without a new law but through something called an 'order'.

'You shouldn't believe stuff you read in the paper,' Carl said to himself, and from the stare a passing woman gave him, he realised he had said it aloud.

CHAPTER SIX

Lizzie Milsom kept hold of Stacey's keys, both sets. No one seemed to know she had them. The police were not long in Stacey's flat, and when they had finally gone, three days after the discovery of the body, Lizzie let herself in once more and walked round the rooms, examining pieces of furniture and equipment, looking at the lovely prints of tropical birds that adorned the walls and confirming that all Stacey's possessions were a lot nicer than anything she had. If she lived here, she wouldn't have to convince herself of her power by borrowing little knick-knacks. She would be powerful already, and confident.

Someone must now be the owner of the flat in Pinetree Court, Lizzie thought, but surely Stacey hadn't left it to anyone? People of twenty-four didn't make wills. It would probably go to her Aunt Yvonne, or a cousin, or even someone who had never heard of Stacey. Lizzie thought she would stay a while, perhaps a few days. No one could get in, she was sure of that, for Stacey had told her there were only two sets of keys: the set Stacey carried in her handbag, and those that were in the outside cupboard. It was possible the concierge had a set, but she wouldn't worry about that.

Lizzie knew she must be careful that no light in the flat was visible from the street below or the car park at the back. The bedroom and bathroom windows looked down on to a kind of tree-shaded yard whose purpose was unclear. The living room was more of a problem, as it fronted on to Primrose Hill Road, but the blinds could be pulled down to cover the window and the curtains drawn to make doubly sure. It was June now, and light till nearly ten, so Lizzie felt pleased with her solution to the problem. She would change and go out, taking both sets of keys with her. It was a pity Stacey had been so overweight – conditioning had made Lizzie never use the word 'fat' – as her clothes would no doubt be a size 16. Yet there Lizzie was only half right, for investigating the left-hand side of the wardrobe as well as the right, she found that ever-hopeful Stacey had kept all or most of the clothes she had worn in her slim days.

Lizzie and Stacey had been the same size in those days, a 10. Lizzie was still a 10. She hunted enjoyably through the clothes and finally laid out on Stacey's bed a jade-green jacket, a very short jade-green skirt and a green and pink top studded with tiny pink pearls. Why not have a bath before getting dressed? Stacey's bath was snow white, wide and deep, a seemingly inexhaustible flood of hot water flowing into it. At home in Kilburn, Lizzie had to rely on a feeble shower that was inclined to splutter, cough and sometimes stop altogether. Soaking in the hot water to which she had added nearly half a bottle of Jo Malone nectarine blossom bath oil, she thought how nice it would be to luxuriate like this every day. Stacey's towels were not towels but bath sheets. Lizzie wrapped herself in one of them, and, having sprayed herself with nectarine scent and dressed in the green ensemble, decided to leave her face fashionably free of make-up. Turning off the lights, she went down in the lift. It was a pleasant summer day, mild and windless. She got into the tube at Swiss Cottage and went the four stops to Willesden Green.

'I've never seen that before,' said her mother when she opened the door. 'Is it new?'

Lizzie said it was, not exactly a lie. The outfit was new to her.

Her parents' house was one of the few in Mamhead Drive not divided into flats. Because it was big, with a large garden, Lizzie had always been proud of it without wanting to go on living there after she came down from university. Tom and Dot Milsom had bought it in 1982 for what Tom now called a derisory sum, and stayed there with no intention of ever moving. Lizzie wandered into the enormous living room, pursued by her mother with cups of tea and cakes on a tray.

'Dad out on a bus?'

'Gone down south today,' said Dot. 'Having a look at some houses in Barnes, he said. I hope he's not thinking of moving.'

'You know he never gets off the bus except to come back,' said Lizzie, thinking of Stacey and refusing a cake her

35

mother called a 'millionaire's macaroon'. She smoothed the
silky stuff of which Stacey's skirt was made and asked her
mother what she thought of the tragedy in Pinetree Court.

When he retired at the age of sixty-five – as he put
it himself, quite a successful man in a small way
– Tom Milsom had never been on a bus. With one assistant, later his partner, he ran a business in commercial
photography from a shop in Willesden he referred to as
an office. It was so near his home in Mamhead Drive
that he could walk to work, and when he was called out
on a job, for a wedding photo, for instance, or – something of a comedown, this – platters of chicken tikka
and lamb biryani for an Indian restaurant chain, he drove
there in the elderly silver Jaguar he kept in pristine
condition. His photographic equipment he carried with
him in the car, and very occasionally, when it needed
servicing or a minor repair, he took his camera and
adjuncts on the tube. Going on a bus he never even
considered. But when the free bus pass for those over
sixty came in, without actually using it he thought it a
waste not to. So he put it in his pocket and forgot it.

Traffic in central London, traffic anywhere in London,
had become what Dot called, using one of her favourite
expressions, 'a nightmare'. And there was nowhere to
park except on the residents' parking in Mamhead Drive
or Dartmouth Place where people didn't need to park
because they had garages of their own. 'Gold dust' in
London, as Dot put it.

Like many men of his age, Tom thought that when he retired, he would find enforced leisure wonderful. He would be free, he would be on a perpetual holiday. What had slipped his mind was how, on the holidays he and Dot had taken over the years, he had been bored stiff trudging along the narrow back streets of little Spanish towns or going on conducted tours to ruined temples in Sicily or trailing up wooded hills in Turkey for the sole purpose of looking at the view from the top. Dot hadn't been bored, or at least had never said she was – but then nor had he said so. She said it was a lovely change from the housework. Tom had no hobbies. He knew nothing about golf; he didn't even watch it on TV. He didn't care for the cinema, which had nothing on it you couldn't get on telly. He had never been much of a reader and had never learned to like classical music. Looking back to those holidays, what he mostly remembered was how slowly the time passed; that when he looked secretly at his watch, thinking it must be eleven thirty by now, he saw it was just ten past ten.

Again like most men, unless they were accompanying a woman, he seldom if ever went to Oxford Street. Dot, who wanted him out of the way one day while she turned out the living room, suggested he go out and buy himself some socks. Possible shops in Willesden she dismissed. Why not go to Oxford Street, where Marks and Spencer – which she, like the rest of the country, called M&S – had their flagship store?

'Go in the car,' she said. 'It won't take you more than half an hour there and back.'

As if saving time was one of his priorities. 'You wouldn't say that if you were a driver.'

Instead of the car, he took the tube, Willesden Green to Bond Street on the Jubilee Line. On a Tuesday morning, Oxford Street wasn't crowded. He bought his socks and walked back towards Bond Street station. If half empty of people, Oxford Street carried a load of buses, so many that Tom fancied their weight would be too much for the road surface and any minute it would crack and sink under this scarlet mass of metal. Where did they all go to? Or come from? Why did they come here, queuing up like animals in a line heading for a water hole? He paused at a bus stop and saw that many buses, six and more if you counted the night ones, were scheduled to stop here. The first on the list was a number 6. He was standing in front of the timetable, which was on a pole and encased in glass, wuhen a bus came looming out of nowhere and bearing down on the bus stop, its light on. The number 6 was on the front of it, and so was its destination: Willesden.

That was the beginning of it, the start of his new occupation. He refused to call it a hobby. Climbing aboard, he waved his pass at the driver, who mimed a touching of this card in a plastic case on to a round yellow disc that squeaked when contact was made. It was easy, it was rather nice. He got a seat near the front and settled down to be driven home for the first time since he'd come to live in Willesden Green.

That was a year ago, and in that year he had ridden at least half of London's buses, been everywhere and become an expert. This afternoon he was coming back from Barnes and in the Marylebone Road had changed on to his favourite number 6. A most interesting afternoon it had been, and outside the sun had come out brilliantly.

Most parents would be delighted to come home and find their grown-up daughter paying an unsolicited visit. Dot evidently was, plying this vision in jade green and rose pink with cups of tea, plates of cakes and now something that was obviously a gin and tonic. Since her late teens, when Tom had expected Lizzie to change, to grow up and behave, he had viewed his daughter with a sinking heart, only briefly pleased when she got into what she called 'uni'. But her degree in media studies was the lowest grade possible while still remaining a BA. Gradually, as she moved from one pathetic job to another, ending up with the one she had now – teaching assistant, alternating with playground supervisor of after-school five-year-olds killing time until a parent came to collect them – he felt for his daughter what no father should feel: a kind of sorrowful contempt. He had sometimes heard parents say of their child that they loved her but didn't like her, and wondered at this attitude. He no longer wondered; he knew. Walking into the house in Mamhead Drive, he asked himself what lie she would tell that evening, and how many justifications for her behaviour she would trot out.

Dot never seemed aware of her lies and prevarications. They had talked about it, of course they had, but such discussions usually ended with Dot saying that she couldn't understand how a father could be so hard on his only child when that child was so devoted to him. As if to prove it, Lizzie got up and kissed him, letting her scented face rest for a moment against his cheek.

Believing he had chosen a subject for conversation unlikely to lead to lying, exaggeration or fantasising, Tom said that Stacey's death had been a sad business. 'I remember her of course from when she was a child in the neighbourhood. You and she used to walk to school together. You and Stacey were good friends.' His wife brought him a glass of wine. 'You'll miss her.'

'Oh yes, I do,' Lizzie said. 'So much. You don't know how much I wish I hadn't been in her flat and found the body. I don't think I could ever set foot in there again.'

'I don't see why you should have to,' said Tom.

'Oh no, I don't have to. I shan't.'

She was lying. He could always tell. He could tell by the tone of her voice and the look on her face, a combination of piety and virtue. They sat down to supper, Lizzie picking delicately at the mushroom omelette that was one of her mother's specialities. Dot wanted to know who owned Stacey's flat now and Lizzie said she had no idea. She wished she did. It was a lovely flat, luxurious and very spacious.

'That's an estate agent's word,' said Tom.

'I couldn't think of another one. What would you say?'

'Roomy,' said Tom.

Lizzie went into detail about how beautiful the flat

was, the carpets, the sleek black and white furniture, the Audubon bird drawings, and this time Tom knew she wasn't lying. Lizzie's love of and knowledge of bird artists and birds themselves was her only intellectual interest. He thought – he couldn't help himself – about the place in Kilburn she lived in and on which he paid half the rent. Nobody would call it beautiful or luxurious, but she was the sole occupant, which was more than you could say for most of her friends, people who shared or had just one room or still lived at home with their parents. He felt hard done by, a state Lizzie's presence usually left him in. She was telling her mother about the shopping spree in Knightsbridge she had been on that had resulted in the purchase of the green suit among other garments. He thought of the portion of her rent he paid, and then, looking at her face, knew that the Knightsbridge story was also a lie and she had spent nothing.

Stacey's flat in Pinetree Court was in darkness when Lizzie got back. She had left the heating on low, and it was very pleasant to be lapped in warmth. She turned on the television to a police drama and went into the bedroom, where she took off the green suit and wrapped herself in the dark blue silk dressing gown she found in Stacey's cupboard. Another cupboard, in the kitchen this time, was well stocked with all kinds of wines and spirits. Lizzie made herself a Tequila Sunrise and settled down in front of the screen with her golden drink.

CHAPTER SEVEN

'Is everything all right between you and Miss Townsend?' said Dermot, passing Carl outside his bedroom door the next morning.

Carl thought this a fearful impertinence. 'Of course it is. Why do you ask?'

'Just being friendly. To tell you the truth, I thought you and she would have put things on a more permanent level by now.'

'What does that mean?'

Dermot smiled, baring his awful teeth. 'Well, once it would have meant marriage, wouldn't it? More like getting engaged these days.'

Carl thought quickly. It wouldn't do to make an enemy of Dermot. 'It takes two to make an engagement,' he said rather gruffly.

Shaking his head, Dermot said, 'I hope I haven't upset you. I wouldn't do that for the world. The way Miss Townsend looks at you, anyone could tell she's crazy about you.' He hesitated, then, 'How about a coffee? Your place or mine?'

'I'll make the coffee,' said Carl, wishing he had said no. 'You won't mind instant?'

'To be perfectly honest with you, I prefer it.'

When Dermot had finally drunk his coffee and gone back upstairs, Carl decided that now was the time to tell Nicola about Stacey. It was Saturday, and she was spending the weekend with her former flatmates. He tried the landline, but there was no reply. Strangely, he couldn't bring himself to try her mobile number. Was it because she would almost certainly answer it?

He needed to talk to Nicola about Stacey, but for some reason, he couldn't. At least not on the telephone. The last time he had gone to dinner with his mother, her friends Jane Porteus and Desmond Jones had been there, and as soon as he came in Jane had begun talking about Stacey and her horrible death. It would be the same with Nicola.

He asked himself why he didn't want to talk about Stacey. He had done nothing wrong; in fact he had been doing her a favour as far as he knew. It wasn't his fault that she had taken an overdose of the pills. She could have checked them on the web. The label had advised using care. All he had done was give her – well, sell her – fifty slimming pills that in some circumstances, for some people, caused nasty symptoms. 'And death,' an inner voice reminded him. Death could be caused by taking DNP. He had by this time been to several dinitrophenol websites, which all mentioned death as a possible result of taking the stuff. Not inevitable, of course, but possible. He had to accept that, painful though it was.

Really, the whole situation was his father's fault. He had died after a heart attack, and one of the websites had said DNP could damage the heart. Could it be . . . ? No, Wilfred had been an old man, and old men died from heart attacks. Young women didn't.

Carl jumped suddenly out of his chair. It was a fine day, another fine day after many in this month of June, and he would go out, walk in the sunshine, think about *Sacred Spirits* and how best to get into it. He had made a false start with this book, and he must begin again. He must find the kind of creative inspiration he had felt when writing *Death's Door*.

He made his way through the little streets of St John's Wood, then turned down Lisson Grove. The June sunshine fell gently on his face, the kind of warmth sunshine should always bestow; not a punishing heat or a mildness spoilt by the wind, but steady and promising a permanence. He thought, why can't I just appreciate things as they come? Why can't I enjoy the moment? I have done nothing wrong. But that inner voice said to him, 'You sold those pills to that girl and you never emphasised to her that they had side effects. You never even told her to google them. You wanted the money. You didn't warn her.'

Nothing, he told himself as he let himself back into his house. There is nothing to be done. Put it out of your mind. Nothing will bring her back. Sit down at that computer and write something. Anything.

*

There must have been close to thirty children in the play centre that afternoon, but on a fine day like this it wasn't so bad looking after kids. Only another half-hour to go and then Lizzie could get back to the beautiful flat in Primrose Hill Road. The playground had been quite a big area when she was a child herself, but over the years it had become smaller as more and more children reached school age, more and more classrooms were needed, as well as a bigger gym and a science lab, though what little kids needed a lab for she didn't know. Now the children actually bumped into each other running about. Lizzie wasn't supposed to have a whistle for the little ones, but she had and blew it often, trying to bring them to heel. Like dogs, said her mother, who didn't approve.

It was worse when it rained and the children had to stay indoors. Another thing Lizzie wasn't supposed to do was feed them with anything but their tea, which consisted of wholemeal bread and Marmite, and apples. Lizzie gave them crisps and sweets called star fruits to shut them up. It cost her a fortune, but it was worth it, especially now she had no gas or electricity to pay for.

On the dot of five thirty, when the parents would start coming for them, she shooed them indoors and counted them. She dreaded one going missing. Not because she cared – if anything, she disliked children – but because of the trouble there would be and the loss of her job. But they were all there today, and they all wanted to get home. So did Lizzie.

It wasn't far to Primrose Hill Road from West End

Lane, just a short walk along Adelaide Road, and halfway along she sat down on a seat, tore up the four slices of wholemeal bread she had taken from the children's snacks and scattered the crumbs on the pavement. Pigeons appeared at once and began gobbling up the bread. People said pigeons were grey, but Lizzie knew better. One was red and green, another was silver with a double streak of snowy white, and a third, perhaps the handsomest, jet black with a metallic emerald sheen to its feathers.

By this time, she had got into Stacey's habit of keeping a set of keys in the recycling cupboard, not because she expected someone else to try to gain entry in her absence – there was no one – but because she was inclined to forget things and knew very well that if she inadvertently shut herself out of Stacey's flat, she would have no means of getting back inside. Not for her the services of a locksmith when she couldn't identify herself as the owner or legal occupant of the flat. No relative had come forward as far as she knew, no other friend who might possess a key. In putting the spare set in the recycling cupboard, in the hollow under the loose brick in the floor, Lizzie calculated she was safe. The only alternative she could think of was to carry the keys with her at all times, maybe on a chain round her neck. She disliked the idea because it spoilt her look when wearing Stacey's clothes.

Una Martin wasn't much of a cook. She relied on smoked salmon and the kind of pasta dishes you bought ready-made and just had to put in the microwave.

Her son didn't notice what he ate and seemed to be glad of anything he got. Una assumed that he and Nicola lived on ready meals and takeaways.

'I've been wondering,' she said as she and Carl began on their first course (there was no second), 'who's going to get poor Stacey's flat? I mean, what happens to property if it's not left to anyone and no one comes forward to claim it?'

'It goes to the Crown,' Carl said, guessing. He didn't really know.

'I've never been in her flat,' Una continued. 'I expect it's very nice.'

'Yes, it is.' Carl helped himself to more pasta. 'I've been a few times.'

'Now if only you'd married her, it would be yours,' said his mother.

Carl sighed. 'I don't need a flat. I've got a nice house. There was no prospect of me marrying her. You got this crazy idea into your head and I don't know where it came from. Stacey was just a friend.'

'There's no such thing as a man and a woman just being friends.'

'Is there any more wine?' Carl asked.

No answer was forthcoming.

'There was an aunt,' he said, remembering.

'What on earth do you mean, darling, there was an aunt?'

'Stacey Warren had an aunt.'

'How do you know?'

'She lived with her after her parents died.'

'So you're saying that this aunt, whoever she is, would inherit that beautiful flat? What's her name? Where does she live?'

'I don't remember,' Carl said, but Una pursued the matter exhaustively. Who was the aunt? How would they find her? How long would it take?

While she talked, Carl sat eating everything that was left. It was a change for him to think about Stacey from a different aspect, not from the point of view of her death and whose fault it was. He also remembered where Stacey had kept her spare set of keys, though he was sure they wouldn't be there any longer.

Una lived in Gloucester Avenue in Camden, which was not far from Primrose Hill Road but some way from the part of it where Stacey's flat was. On a whim, he made a detour on his way home and, looking up at what had been Stacey's windows, saw a faint light on. Someone was in there. Perhaps a solicitor? An estate agent? At twenty minutes to ten at night? It wasn't his business. He had come to check on the keys in the recycling cupboard.

There was no one about. He shifted the recycling bin a few inches, surprised to find it half full of news-papers and packaging. The keys were there all right, underneath the floor brick. Suppose he went up in the lift and let himself into the flat – he had never done so in the past – and found Stacey in there, not as she had been in recent months, but a slim and beautiful ghost, waiting for him, waiting to accuse him of killing her.

Don't be a fool, he said to himself as he made his way out on to Chalk Farm Road, where the pubs were spilling out and noisy crowds sat at the tables on the pavement.

CHAPTER EIGHT

Tom Milsom got off the number 98 bus at Marble Arch and, having walked a few yards to the top of Park Lane, hopped on to the 414. It was amazing how you could get on and off buses and on again all for free. Well, not really free; you'd paid for it in taxes all your life. But he wondered if there was any other capital city in the world where, so long as you were over sixty, you could ride on any bus without paying. He felt a surge of affection for his country, so cruelly maligned by many people. The words of the hymn came into his head, 'I vow to thee, my country, all earthly things above', and tears pricked the back of his eyes, but they were tears of warmth and love.

He went to the upper level. Most people of his age didn't, but you saw so much from the top of a bus, especially when charging down the sloping part of Park Lane. He looked down at the Dorchester and Grosvenor House and the beautiful houses that remained, and there, walking along the pavement, was his next-door neighbour Mrs Grenville, holding the hand of a man who wasn't her husband. Tom thought it should have been a woman observing this bit of scandal; gossip was wasted on him.

It was three in the afternoon, and the bus was three-quarters empty as it made its way down into Knightsbridge. To his surprise, it stopped right outside Harrods. No use to him, he thought. He might as well stay on and go to the bus's destination, Putney Bridge. There was bound to be another bus waiting there for him, one he had never been on before, never even heard of, and if it didn't take him all the way home, it would take him somewhere he could pick up a number 98 or even a 6, which passed the end of Mamhead Drive.

Carl was forcing himself to write three or four paragraphs every day, but now as he read his new pages, he admitted to himself that they weren't very good. The prose was laboured, heavy, lifeless, the obvious result of pushing himself. But it's about a philosopher, he thought, it's bound not to have the witty lightness of *Death's Door*. Perhaps he should look on his efforts as a practice run, a trial exercise to get himself back into novelist mode? He produced a few more lines and interrupted himself by remembering that today was the last of the month and tomorrow the first of July, rent day. Of course the rent wouldn't come; it never now came the day before, though apologies sometimes did.

So he wasn't surprised when Dermot tapped at his door. Letting him in, he awaited the excuses. But there were no excuses, only smiles and the handover of a brown envelope.

'What's this, then?'

'Your rent, Carl. What else?'

'You never pay me the day before,' said Carl, 'or the day itself, come to that.' He opened the envelope and took out the so-desirable purple notes. 'Still, I'm not complaining.'

'Look at it this way. It may be the first time, but it may also be the last.'

'You don't mean you're leaving?'

'Oh, no. No, no.'

Dermot gave Carl another of his ghastly smiles, the yellow blotches on his teeth looking worse than usual. Carl noticed that a large pustule had appeared on his chin. He listened to him mounting the stairs, and then asked himself what that had meant. That stuff about Dermot's payment being the last.

It meant nothing, he told himself. Dermot thought he was being funny. Put it out of your head. It was nonsense.

But that 'no, no' rang out and echoed in his head. He looked again at the contents of the envelope. Perhaps there were twice as many notes this month? But he had counted them the first time and there were not. He wanted to get back to *Sacred Spirits*, but concentration was impossible.

'Oh, no. No, no' surely meant that Dermot wasn't giving up his flat. It had been a very firm denial. Suddenly Carl saw that, firm or not, it had nothing to do with the contents of the envelope being Dermot's last payment.

He had plainly said it might be the last. Could he have meant instead that at the end of next month, there would be no envelope and no money? He couldn't mean that. A tenant had to pay his rent. He would have to ask Dermot what he had meant. He couldn't go another four weeks with the suspense of not knowing.

But a week went by without Carl doing anything about it. From his living room window he saw Dermot going off to work, and on the Sunday morning leaving for church. Some respite from the nagging anxiety came with the idea that Dermot had only meant that this was the last time the twelve hundred pounds would be paid in cash, and that in future he intended to pay by cheque or direct debit. The relief lasted only a few minutes. If he had meant that, he would have said so.

Carl had rarely been to the top floor since Dermot had arrived. Now he determined to go up and ask for an explanation of their last bizarre exchange. What had it meant? Ten days had passed since he had encountered Dermot. Almost never in the course of their association – you couldn't call it a friendship – had as much as ten days gone by without their seeing each other, even if only on the stairs.

He left it another two days. There was still no sign of Dermot. But he wasn't ill and confined to bed, and he hadn't done a moonlight flit. Carl could occasionally hear footfalls on the bare boards of the top-floor flat, and once a burst of religious music indicated that Dermot's front door was open. On the third day after he had come to his decision, he climbed the top flight and thumped on the door

'Goodness me,' said Dermot from inside. 'Whatever's wrong? Has something happened?'

'Just open the door, will you?'

The door came open, but slowly, rather reluctantly, as if it had been bolted on the inside. There had never been bolts on that door before Dermot came. From the kitchen came a strong smell of sausages and bacon frying. Stepping back to let Carl come in, Dermot said in the pleasantest, friendliest tone he had ever heard from him, 'Now I do hope there isn't going to be trouble, Carl. We have had such an amicable relationship up till now.'

'I just want you to tell me something.'

'If I can. You know I always bend over backwards to keep a peaceful atmosphere. Now what can I tell you? No, wait, let me make us a nice cup of coffee.'

'I don't want any bloody coffee,' said Carl. 'I want you to tell me what you meant when you handed me the last lot of rent. You said it was the first time and it might be the last. I said, "You're not leaving, are you?" and you said, "Oh, no. No, no."'

Dermot smiled his ghastly smile, said, 'Let me just pop into the kitchenette while I turn off the burner.' He came back still smiling. 'There, sorry about that. I couldn't have my lunch ruined, could I? Yes, back to our last conversation. I don't quite see where I went wrong. I said I wasn't leaving, and I'm not. Does that satisfy you? Not leaving. Staying. Happy again?'

Carl felt rage rising inside him. Dermot was playing

with him. 'Correct me if I'm wrong, but we have an agreement, signed by both of us, and witnessed. Right? And that agreement states that you pay me a certain sum each month while you occupy this flat. Right again?'

Dermot had put a spoonful of instant coffee into each of two mugs and picked up the electric kettle. Through a window in the side of the kettle Carl could see the water boiling. Dermot held it very close to Carl's face, and Carl flinched, jerking his chair back. Smiling, Dermot poured water on to the coffee.

'Ah, but don't you remember who the witness was? I do. It was Stacey Warren. A sheet of paper taken out of your printer, written on by you and witnessed by a woman who's now passed away. Valueless, I'd say, wouldn't you?' Dermot took a gulp of the strong black coffee he had made. It would have choked Carl but it had almost no effect on the other man. 'So yes, I'm staying, but I'd say it's probable I'll never pay you rent again.'

'But you can't live here rent-free.'

'I think I can,' said Dermot very calmly. 'Shall I tell you why? It's DNP. Dinitrophenol. I think you should know that while I'm a believer, a pretty strict follower of the Christian faith, a churchgoer, as you may have noticed, I haven't any of what some people call honour. Now I know you had a cabinetful of DNP. It came from your dad, I heard you say, and I had a good scrounge round through all his medication. If you didn't want that happening you should have locked your bathroom door. The first time there were a hundred capsules, the second time fifty. You sold fifty of those poisonous pills to Stacey

Warren, didn't you? As a matter of fact, I was passing your open bathroom door when the transaction – the sale, I mean – took place.'

Carl would have expected someone in his situation to turn white. They did in books. In his own book. Conversely, his face had flushed, and he could feel the skin burning.

'It's not against the law. It's not. You can't make it against the law,' he said in a tremulous voice, a voice that didn't sound like his own,

Without a word, Dermot got up and walked out of the room. He was back quickly, carrying a page cut from the *Guardian*. 'You want to read that. You can keep it. I've got copies.'

Killed by DNP, the line under the pictures said, photographs of a girl and a young man and a number of yellow capsules. The police believed that the man had given the pills to the girl with the specific intention of killing her. He had used DNP as a poison. Carl read in the article that the drug could kill even if doses of it had been safely taken previously. One woman had taken it for two years before she died. Another's death had been mysterious until tests found that the pills by her bed were DNP. The drug was available online, and selling it wasn't against the law, but it could too easily be lethal. Two MPs had expressed concern, and one said it might be helpful to have DNP brought under the Misuse of Drugs Act.

Carl laid down the paper. He was sweating and could feel the drops of perspiration on his upper lip. 'This means nothing. The drug is not illegal.'

'So you're not worried,' said Dermot. 'In two weeks' time I pay your rent and you won't mind if I chat to a few people about what you did. Fifty pills. That's a lot. More than enough to kill. Perhaps you intended her to die? And what about your reputation as a brilliant young writer, such a promising new talent?'

Carl stood up. 'So you want to chat to people about me? That's rich. And who are these people?'

'Sit down a minute. There's the press, of course. The anonymous tip here and there. And I've been doing my homework. Stacey Warren had an aunt, and this aunt has a son and a daughter. As it happens, I know the aunt quite well. Mrs Yvonne Weatherspoon was devoted to Stacey, and had her to stay when her parents died. She brings her cat to the clinic where I work, and it would be the easiest thing in the world to have a little chat with her about poor Stacey's death. In fact she's due to bring the cat in for her shots tomorrow.'

Carl knew very well that you should never say 'How dare you?' to anyone, least of all someone who was threatening you. It sounded ridiculous. But he did say it. 'How dare you threaten me, you blackmailer?'

But Dermot seemed very calm and in command of the situation. 'I've been threatening you for the past ten minutes, as you very well know. I can't threaten you with police arrest. But it's nasty stuff, isn't it? Mrs Weatherspoon is a very strong-minded woman – do they still use that expression? You probably know better than I do. A strong character is what I mean. Once she knows where poor Stacey got the DNP, she will, as they say, take it further.

The *Hampstead and Highgate Express*, for a start, and maybe that paper that operates around Muswell Hill? They may even send their photographer round to get a picture of you. Stacey was well known. You're a novelist. The gossip columns will love it.'

'I don't want to talk any more about it,' said Carl. 'You have to pay the rent and that's all there is to it.'

He was barely out of the room when he heard his tenant putting the coffee cups in the sink and tipping the contents of the frying pan on to a plate.

Without that rent, what was he going to live on? It would take him months, if not years, to finish *Sacred Spirits*, and already he had no confidence in his work. But this was all hypothetical. He would have his rent and let that criminal bastard, that blackmailer, do his worst. He would ignore him. He would get back to his writing.

This brave stance buoyed Carl for a while. But when he sat down at the computer again, he found that nothing would come. All he wrote, without really knowing that he was doing so, were the words that kept running in a continuous loop through his head: *it's not against the law, it's not against the law, it's not against the law.*

CHAPTER NINE

The Sutherland Pet Clinic was within easy walking distance of Falcon Mews. Dermot could be there in less than ten minutes. Like St Matthew, who was a kind of tax collector, he sat at the receipt of custom, but unlike the saint, since there was no animal welfare in the Holy Land, he made appointments and received payment for neutering, injections, operations, check-ups and, sadly, euthanasia. It was not unknown for Dermot to bow his head and weep a little when Jake or Honey had to be put to sleep. That was the terminology he preferred; he had been known to admonish a cat or dog owner who spoke of 'putting down' an animal.

The area of his job he liked best was as a salesman, such as when he was called upon to advise a client about which variety of cat food he would recommend for sixteen-year-old Mopsy or kitten Lucy. Which artificial bones would he suggest for the incorrigible biter Hannibal or breath deodorant for ancient Pickwick? His finest contribution to the social life of the clinic was the Pet of the Month competition he had invented. This was very popular. Owners submitted their pet's details to him with a photograph and some instances of bravery or achievement, and he judged which was the top dog or cat. Up on the wall for the rest of this month was a charming photograph of Pippa, a cuddly British Blue whose howls at midnight had alerted her owners to the presence of a burglar in the house. The announcement of the competition winner he timed – so that he couldn't forget it – for his rent day. This of course would no longer be a factor, so he would have to fix on some other way of remembering to reveal the result.

The day after his encounter with Carl, Dermot was sitting behind his desk at the clinic, contemplating the list of clients expected that day, when Yvonne Weatherspoon arrived with Sophonisba, her Maine Coon, in her cat box. Her appointment was for nine thirty and it was now twenty past. Sophonisba, always called Sophie, was due for a flea and worm check.

Close on fifty but retaining her fine blonde good looks and slender figure, Yvonne had already confided in the sympathetic Dermot about her niece's death, hugging Sophie and squeezing out a tear or two.

'You know who I'm talking about, don't you, Dermot?'

'Ah, yes. That poor young lady Miss Stacey Warren, the beautiful actress. What a sad event that was.'

'Well, we were very close, you know.' Dermot did know, but continued to listen with great interest. 'She left me her flat. Well, she didn't actually leave it to me, but I am her next of kin, her heir. I'm not going to live in it. I've already got a lovely house of my own, what the

62

government calls a mansion, and dear Sophie wouldn't put up with moving. Cats hate a change of home, as I'm sure you know.'

'Yes, indeed.'

'I'm going to hand it over to my son Gervaise. He and poor Stacey were very close.'

'He's a very fortunate young man,' said Dermot.

Further conversation was terminated by the appearance of Caroline, the head vet, come to fetch Yvonne and Sophie. The cat, no doubt aware of what was in store for her, set up a howling, and Dermot, left to his thoughts, said a thank you to God, but in a whisper, because the deity could hear everything.

The thanks to the Almighty were not for the outcome of his interview with Carl, but for the news imparted by Yvonne Weatherspoon. Carl already knew about Dermot's acquaintance with Yvonne, but not that her son was moving into Stacey's flat. And this knowledge would confirm to him something that Dermot was sure Carl had doubted: that at almost any time, and in an intimate manner, he could impart the details of the DNP sale to Yvonne. Perhaps, if he could fix it, he could also tell Gervaise, he who had been so close to 'poor Stacey'.

Carl had called him a blackmailer. Dermot hadn't liked that. Not at all. He didn't see himself that way. You could almost say he was the reverse of a blackmailer, because instead of taking money from Carl as the price of his silence, he was withholding it. He had never disliked Carl, and didn't now. To dislike anyone would be unchristian. To love your neighbour as yourself was a tenet of his faith, and Dermot was proud of loving himself a lot. In any case, there was nothing in the Bible about blackmail. Or reverse blackmail.

The street door opened and Mr Sanderson came in with his Dalmatian, Spots. Not Spot, but the plural – 'Because he's got lots of them,' the dog's owner had once said. 'I counted, and there were a hundred and twenty-seven.'

Very privately, Dermot thought all the clients were mad.

Carl was forcing himself to write. He read and reread what he had written, and tinkered with words, but with no noticeable effect. He was writing stiffly: the little dialogue he attempted was stilted and strangely outdated, and his characters spoke to each other as if they lived in the middle of the last century.

The reason for his failings was obvious. His mind was full of Dermot's threat to withhold the rent or ruin his reputation. The rent was due on 31 July, though in the usual course of things it would not be brought to him until the first or second day of August. Would it be brought at all this time? Would Dermot carry through on his threat? Carl had avoided his tenant since their conversation, but he often heard his footsteps on the stairs. He thought about him constantly, and if he could manage to fall asleep at all, he woke in the small hours and stayed awake for the rest of the night, tossing and turning and no doubt disturbing Nicola, creating all possible variations on what would happen if the rent didn't come, what he would do and what Dermot would do.

He had said nothing about Dermot's threat to Nicola, reasoning that if he told her, he would also have to tell her about selling the DNP to Stacey. He should have told her long ago. She knew that something was worrying him. Would she understand? Nicola was almost indifferent to money, seldom bought clothes like other girls did, never used make-up. Unlike the other women he knew, she was always reading books – books made of paper, not cyberspace – and listening to what he called classical music and she called real music. That was one reason he had been attracted to her. She had loved *Death's Door*. She was his biggest fan. So why hadn't he told her about Stacey?

The longer he waited, the more difficult it became. Once, anticipating her return from work at six thirty, he found himself wishing she hadn't moved in. He reproached himself for that, telling himself that this dread would pass, that one day it would be gone but he would still have her.

'I don't believe you've got any food in the house,' she'd said the previous evening. 'I think you've lost weight, and you can't afford that.' A note of anxiety came into her voice. 'You look as if you've been ill, which you haven't, I know.'

'I've been a bit under the weather,' he said, in Dermot mode.

On the way back from doing the shopping together, he thought he might tell her. He'd make her promise not to tell anyone, and once he'd got that undertaking from her, he'd confide in her, tell her everything he'd done, starting with the collection of medicines and remedies he had inherited from his father. She had, of course, seen them in the bathroom they shared, but they had never discussed them. Then he'd go on to talk about Stacey and her weight, her despair and how she had begged him to let her have the yellow capsules. If he put it like that, Nicola would see how impossible it'd been for him to refuse.

'You're very quiet,' she said now. 'You really are worrying about something, aren't you? I've sensed it for a while.'

'I'll be all right.'

'As soon as we get home, we'll have a glass of that Chablis. We could both do with it. I've had a bit of a rough day.'

Not compared to his day, Carl thought, or the eleven or twelve days he'd lived through since Dermot threatened him. And as he thought of Dermot, as they made their way into Falcon Mews, his tenant approached from the other end. He was walking jauntily, in Carl's eyes, and carrying tulips.

'Snap!' said Dermot, and to Nicola, 'What a coincidence. Long time since we've seen you round this neck of the woods.'

Carl muttered to himself that he had never before seen a man buy flowers for himself, but Dermot didn't hear because Nicola was telling him how nice it was to see him. She was out all day and their paths never seemed to cross. They let him go into the house first. Carl was thinking with longing of that glass of Chablis. He seldom bought wine. He had let Nicola buy two bottles, explaining in the shop that he couldn't afford it, though he still had some money from this month's rent. But was it the last he would receive?

Nicola put the food in the fridge and poured the wine generously. 'Waiters and barmen always fill your glass only half full. Have you noticed? It never used to be like that.'

He didn't say anything. He could hear Dermot pacing around two floors up. It sounded as if he was leaping up and down. He took his wine into the living room.

'Shall we have some music, Carl? I've bought you a new CD.'

'Not yet,' he said. 'I've got something to tell you.'

The face she turned to him was aghast. It was the only possible word.

'No, no. Nothing that's going to affect you,' he said. 'For God's sake, don't look like that.' He set his glass down, hesitated, and then picked it up again to take a great gulp of his wine. Seated now on the sofa, he patted the cushion beside him; when she sat down, he took her face in his hands and kissed her with a gentleness that surprised even him. 'There,' he said. 'I don't know what you'll think. And better not say a word to Dermot after what I tell you; I mean, if you felt like going up there and having it out with him.'

'What is it?'

'It has to do with Stacey Warren. You didn't really know her, did you?'

'I'd met her, of course. She was your friend. Is that what's been bothering you? Her death?'

He waited for her to say how fat Stacey had become, but she didn't.

'Nicola, you know those medicines – well, I suppose you'd call them quack remedies – my dad left in the house? Stacey came to see me one day, and she found these pills. Well, capsules. They're called dinitrophenol.' It sounded better using that word, as Nicola might have read the name in the newspaper. 'I didn't know anything about the pills, but she said they could help her lose weight. She asked me if she could have some.'

Nicola took a sip of her wine.

'There were about a hundred in the packet. I let her have fifty.' An idea came to him. 'Would you like to see them? I've still got the rest.'

Nicola nodded. They went upstairs and she followed him into the bathroom. He took the packet of yellow capsules out of the cupboard and she held it in her hand. 'You gave her fifty?'

There was no point in telling her at all if he failed to tell her the truth. So why was it so hard? He looked into her beautiful, gentle face. It would be fine; she just wanted clarification. 'As a matter of fact, I sold them to her. A pound each, that's the price that was listed on the package.' Nicola nodded, but gave no indication what she was nodding about. She handed back the capsules and walked out of the room. He went after her, but she moved slowly. On the stairs, she turned and said over her shoulder, 'And she died? Did she die because of the dinitro-whatever?'

'They said at the inquest that it contributed to her death. Come back and finish your wine, and then we can make supper.'

'Where does Dermot come into it?'

He saw now that bringing his tenant in would make things much worse. Should he tell her that Dermot was threatening him? Instead, he repeated the phrase: 'The pills are not against the law.'

'Then they should be,' she said.

'Maybe.' He began to reel off the stories he had taken from the newspapers of people who had used DNP and lost weight but been OK. Their temperatures had risen dangerously and they had felt very ill but they'd got thin and now they were absolutely fine. 'Please, can we have another drink?'

'Not for me.'

'What's wrong, Nic?'

There was no need to ask. The tears were falling silently down her cheeks. He had never seen her cry before. 'Why are you crying?'

'You know. Of course you do. I love you, or I thought I did. But I don't think I can love someone who did what you did. Gave her pills – sold her pills – that you must have known were dangerous. It's horrible.'

Carl shook his head. 'I'm not hearing this.'

'Yes you are. Don't you see it was bad enough giving her the stuff, let alone selling it to her?' She wiped her eyes with a tissue. 'I can't believe you've kept all this a secret from me. I should never have come to live here.'

'Don't go, Nic. Please don't go.'

'I've nowhere to go to. The girls have let my room in the flat. I'll have to sleep in the spare room.'

Carl had never felt such despair. It enclosed him in its cold emptiness. He drank about half the second of the bottles of wine they had bought – no, Nicola had bought. He went into the kitchen and ate a slice of bread and a hunk of cheese. It seemed that he lived on bread and cheese these days. Later, after he had slept a while on Dad's sofa, he heard Nicola getting ready for bed, using the bathroom, fetching herself a glass of water. He held his breath, hoping against hope that she had changed her mind and gone into their bedroom. But no, she hadn't.

The spare bedroom door creaked a little when it closed, and now he heard the creak before the click of the lock.

CHAPTER TEN

The flat in Pinetree Court could never become her permanent home; Lizzie knew this from the moment she moved herself in there. She had known it when she discovered Stacey's body. But the trouble was, she was getting accustomed to it. It had begun to feel like hers. She even cleaned it, which was the first time she had ever cleaned anywhere. Her mother came round and hoovered and dusted her place in Kilburn, but the flat in Pinetree Court was so beautiful, so luxurious, that Lizzie couldn't bear the idea of its getting dirty, so she did it herself.

She wondered why no one had taken the place over. It was weeks since Stacey had died, and it must by now belong to someone. It must have been *left* to someone. Perhaps the person it had been left to didn't want to live there because he or she had a place of their own. Lizzie tried to think who besides Stacey's Aunt Yvonne this person might be. Stacey had once been Carl Martin's sort of girlfriend, or had been till she got so obese, but though Lizzie had known Carl years ago, they had not had any contact recently. She couldn't really go up to him in the street and ask him what was happening to Stacey's flat. And he probably wouldn't know anyway.

But what about that chap who lived in the top half of what she had heard from Stacey was Carl's house? Lizzie liked walking through the mews, imagining what it would be like to live there. One time she'd seen that chap come out of the front door. This was before she'd started at the school and when she'd been doing old Miss Phillips's typing. Imagine being called 'Miss' in this day and age! One day Lizzie had to take Miss Phillips's pooch, a very fat pug, to the vet's and there was that chap from Falcon Mews on reception. Was he a vet, then? No matter; she would think of a reason to go into the clinic and ask him whether by any chance he knew if Carl now owned a flat in Pinetree Court.

Lizzie was going out to dinner with a new man. She'd met him at a coffee bar near Stacey's flat. He seemed posh, promising, though she couldn't yet call him her boyfriend. His name was Swithin Campbell. She was meeting him at Delaunay's in the West End, and afterwards he would bring her back here in a taxi and she would ask him in for coffee or something out of one of those exotic bottles of Stacey's. She had never before met anyone called Swithin; she had only heard of it in connection with St Swithin's Day. Sometime in July it was, and if it rained that day (it always did), it would keep on raining for forty days, or so her father said.

Lizzie never went to hairdressers. She had thick, glossy

caramel-coloured hair that only needed washing. She put on what she judged to be Stacey's best dress, more a gown than a dress, and in a gorgeous blue-green colour. It was called teal, Lizzie thought, and the neckline was encrusted with what looked like turquoises. She had bought nail varnish in the same colour on the way back from the playgroup but decided against it. Men only liked red varnish.

At ten to seven, she went downstairs to walk to Chalk Farm tube station. She was trying not to spend money on taxis.

Tom Milsom had had a lovely day, down to Holborn on the number 98, lunch in a nice pub where they served very good fish and chips, then back on the 139, which didn't go where he thought it would, but dropped him outside a tube station that happened to be on the Jubilee line. The train took him to Willesden Green. Then it was just a short walk to Mamhead Drive.

Dot had wanted to come with him, but he had put her off, he hoped not unkindly. He said she would be bored, but the truth was that he enjoyed his bus trips so much, he wanted to keep them to himself. He didn't want to talk but to look and, he supposed, to learn, to discover how little he really knew of London. Now he *was* learning, and that was something she wouldn't understand. She and Lizzie tended to laugh at this new interest of his, but to him it wasn't funny. It was marvellous, and very serious.

Next week he would be more ambitious. He could take the number 6 to halfway down the Edgware Road, then get on the 7. Lizzie had once told him that she went on that bus to the Portobello Road. It was such a trendy place to go to that he hadn't liked to tell her he had never been there, that he barely knew where it was. The number 7 bus driver would, though.

'You're very quiet,' Dot said when he got in. 'Thinking about your exciting trip, are you? I'll come with you one of these days.'

'No you won't,' Tom said hastily. 'You don't get your pass till you're sixty.'

The following day he took the number 16 to Victoria. The building works going on around the bus station, the chaos and the crowds, even though it was only half past three in the afternoon, made him resolve not to come here again until the underground improvement works were finished.

Coming home, he got on the 16, which went to Cricklewood Broadway, from where he could transfer to one of the three routes that would take him to Willesden. But at the Edgware Road stop, a big burly man got on, slapped his pass on to the card reader and shouted out when it didn't beep. The driver took the card from him and read it; it was out of date and he told the fat man he would need to renew it. The queue getting on the bus began muttering angrily. The man with the out-of-date pass shouted insults at the driver, calling him a black bastard. That was enough. The driver said to get off, everyone must get off because he was calling the police. The man with the out-of-date pass yelled that he wasn't getting off, and the driver said good, that suited him. Tom escaped through the exit in the middle of the bus and walked the short distance to the next stop, where he got on the number 6.

He smiled. When he got home, he would tell Dorothy about the row on the bus. She always enjoyed a bit of a fight so long as no one came to blows.

For once, as Lizzie put it to herself, she hadn't drunk very much, just a gin and tonic and two small glasses of wine the whole evening. She wanted to make a good impression on Swithin, and she noticed how little he drank.

He had seemed at their first meeting an intelligent man, but he hadn't much conversation, and long silences fell. She tried to fill the gaps by telling him about her father's bus rides, making his small adventures as amusing as she could, but he appeared to have no sense of humour. Like most of her friends, Lizzie believed that if a man took you out for an expensive dinner in a place such as this one, he would expect you to have sex with him afterwards. Of course you didn't necessarily have to. She looked across the table at him and smiled mysteriously. He began talking about the Scottish referendum.

Taking her home in a taxi, he accepted her invitation to come in for coffee. She had only once tried Stacey's espresso machine and looked forward to using it again.

She wanted to see the impression it made on him. She wasn't disappointed.

'You own this place, do you?'

Those were almost his first words as he walked into the living room. She said she did.

'At current prices it must be worth close on a million.'

'Not quite that,' she said and went to make the coffee. When she came back, he was looking at Stacey's paintings of tropical birds and examining a table of pale yellow wood with a grey inlay. Lizzie didn't much like it; it was the kind of thing her mother would have called too modern.

'Is it a ——?' Swithin uttered a name that sounded like a town in Slovakia.

'Oh yes. It was very pricey.' She knew she shouldn't have said that. It wasn't the sort of word to use in connection with valuable furniture. 'I didn't buy it, my mother did.'

He gave her a strange look. They drank their coffee and he talked about house prices. When he had emptied his cup, she expected him to move towards her along the sofa, but he got up instead. 'Very good coffee,' he said.

There was nothing to say to that. He gave her a kiss, a light peck on the cheek, and quickly departed.

In the weeks she had been in Pinetree Court, few callers had come to the door. The post, what there was of it, was deposited in the boxes in the entrance hall. Meters were read in cupboards outside and by the front doors. So when the doorbell rang the following morning, Lizzie jumped. She wasn't going to answer it or even guess who it might be. It rang again. It will ring twice, she thought, and then they'll give up and go away.

The sound of a key turning in the lock brought a cold shiver. She waited in the little hallway as a man she recognised as the concierge stepped into the flat. With him was a tall, very handsome man of about her own age whom she vaguely recognised.

'Who might you be?' said the concierge.

Lizzie did her best to make her voice bold. 'I'm a friend of Miss Warren's. I'm looking after the place.'

'Miss Warren passed away some time ago. The apartment is now about to be occupied by this gentleman, Mr Weatherspoon.'

Of course. That was who it was. Aunt Yvonne's son.

'Hi, Gervaise,' said Lizzie.

'Well, if it isn't little Lizzie,' said Gervaise Weatherspoon. 'How did you get in?'

'I've had a key for *years*,' she said.

It was plain the concierge didn't believe her, something Lizzie resented, as for once what she said was more or less true. 'I'll have that key, thank you, miss, and then we'll say no more about it,' he said.

She gave him the key meekly because she had just remembered she didn't need it. The other one, the one in the floor of the recycling cupboard, was known to her and her alone. She favoured Gervaise with a radiant smile. 'Will you be living here?'

'One day,' he said with a smile to match hers. 'First

I'll be going on an archaeological visit to Cambodia and Laos.'

Gervaise asked for Lizzie's phone number so she could give him details of the flat's phone and energy suppliers. The concierge looked disgruntled: he could help Mr Weatherspoon with that, he said. But Lizzie took no notice and wrote down her mobile number and the landline at the Kilburn flat. Gervaise's request had given her an idea, and done her a power of good. Never mind that she was going to be an hour late for school.

'I'll be in touch,' she promised.

Lizzie packed every bag she could find in the flat. Seeing no reason to leave any of Stacey's clothes behind, she stuffed them into suitcases from Louis Vuitton, Marks & Spencer and Selfridges. Then she phoned for a taxi.

While she was waiting for it, there came a knock at the door. Of course she thought it was the taxi, but no, it was the concierge, with an enormous bunch of white lilies, feathery gypsophila and pink rosebuds. The card accompanying it was addressed to 'Darling Liz' with love from Swithin. Liz indeed. No one had ever called her that.

Taking the flowers with her, she removed the extra key from underneath the brick in the floor of the recycling cupboard and put it in her handbag. Then she stacked the luggage on the pavement to wait for the taxi to take her to Kilburn.

CHAPTER ELEVEN

Rent day, the last day of the month, had gone past. By 2 August, Carl knew he wouldn't be paid.

He wasn't yet destitute. The second instalment of the advance he had received on publication of *Death's Door* had taught him to be careful, if not frugal, and though nearly all of that had gone, he had saved a little more from the July rent that had come in. He probably had as much as four hundred pounds in his current account. But if Dermot's August rent failed to appear – and plainly it was not going to – the demand for council tax did. *City of Westminster* it said across the top of the letter, and underneath that, the sum. He could pay it in instalments, of course, but was that much help?

That afternoon, he sat down at the computer, went to the document called *Sacred Spirits*.doc, and read with mounting disgust what he had written. It was hopeless, useless. Tinkering with it was a waste of time. After staring at the text in despair, he deleted all ten pages. He must forget this philosophy theme, this learned stuff he was obviously useless at, and think seriously of something he could do, like a sequel to *Death's Door*. If that wasn't feasible, he could create a new detective, a woman, perhaps. He would begin by making a list of characters, looking up names online and finding new ones in the surname dictionary.

But his heart wasn't in it. All his heart could do was sink. He missed Nicola so much. Her old flatmates had found room for her. She was gone. And there was Dermot. Suppose he really did stay in the flat and never paid the rent again? Perhaps Carl could tell him to leave because he wanted to sell the house. But he knew this wouldn't work. Dermot would refuse to go.

There was another course to follow. Force him to pay the rent and leave him to do his worst. Dermot would no doubt tell this woman Yvonne Weatherspoon the tale of Carl's 'medicaments' and the sale of the DNP to Stacey. And why should it stop there? Dermot might not lead an involved and widespread social life, but he met a lot of people. He talked (chatted, he would call it) to a host of pet-owners, for example. He would carry out his threat to go to that newspaper that sold widely in Hampstead and Highgate. He would say he had a story for them and go to their office to give an interview. He might even approach one of the tabloids, the *Sun*, say, or the *Mail*. Stacey was known to the public. It would be a juicy story: 'Author Kills Actress'. Carl would never have a serious literary career again.

He was making himself feel sick. He leaned over his desk, putting his head in his hands, but this did nothing to help. He ran, choking, into the kitchen and threw up into the sink.

The footsteps behind him could only be Dermot's. Carl kept his head bent, ran the cold tap, switched on the waste disposal unit, hoping the noise would drive his tenant away. It didn't.

'You're not very well, are you?' Dermot used his deeply concerned voice. To Carl it sounded as if he was enjoying himself. 'Don't you think you should see your doctor? I'll come with you if you like.'

'Go away. You're ruining my life.'

'No, no,' said Dermot. 'It's you who's doing that.'

Carl drank some water from the tap. He wiped his mouth on the tea cloth.

Dermot said, 'I came down to ask you if you would like to go out for a drink. Maybe something to eat as well?'

This was an instance when to respond with 'Are you joking?' was a genuine question.

'No,' Dermot said. 'I thought it would be a good idea to get to know each other better.'

Carl said, 'I don't want to know you better. I don't want to know you at all. I want you out of my life. Now go away, please. Please go away.'

When Dermot had gone, Carl sat down at the kitchen table, found Nicola's mother's number on his phone's list of contacts and rang it. There was no answer. He remembered his own mother telling him that there was a time not so long ago when your name didn't come up when you made a call. The person you called didn't know who it was, so they had to answer. As things were now, Nicola might be sitting in her mother's house, also in a kitchen for all he knew, and deliberately not answering because she could see 'Carl' on the screen. He thought, I don't even know where her house is. Aylesbury, I think, but I don't know the address.

As he was leaving, the postman brought ten copies of Carl's book. When he'd originally been shown the jacket design he hadn't liked it, but had accepted the corpse and the blood and the weeping woman. It looked no better now under the bright-coloured glaze, and he dumped the box on the hall table and left it there. A moment in time that should have been glorious – the delivery of copies of his first published book – was just a disappointment, like everything else in his life.

He decided to walk to Nicola's flat in Ashmill Street, telling himself he'd nothing to lose if no one let him in. Things couldn't be any worse than they already were. It occurred to him that he had no one to talk to, no one to confide in. There was only Nicola, and perhaps even she wouldn't speak to him.

He walked through Church Street market, where the traders were dismantling the stalls. Further up on Lisson Grove, the man with the antique shop was removing his chairs and tables from the pavement and closing up for the night.

By now it was early evening, and once off the main streets, few people were about. Carl turned down the street by the fish and chip shop. Nicola knew, he said to himself. She was the only one other than Dermot who knew; she had heard his account of what had happened, she *knew*. Surely now she would be over her initial shock and horror and would be able to give him some sympathy, tell him what to do.

The Victorian terraced house where she lived was one of a long row, and must have been ugly and shabby even when it was first built. It looked empty, as if all the girls were out somewhere; with friends, maybe, or boyfriends, having coffee or a drink or at the cinema. Nicola wouldn't be there, he accepted this, but one of the others might know where she was. He rang the bell, the top bell for the top floor, then rang it again.

The window above him opened and Nicola put her head out.

'Let me in, Nic. Please.'

She smiled her beautiful Nicola smile. 'I'm coming down.'

It wasn't all right, it couldn't be that, but it was better. He knew it was better when, as soon as she had let him in and closed the front door, she took him in her arms and hugged him tightly. He felt like a small child whose mother had been cross with him for some misdemeanour, but had now forgiven him and loved him again as she used to.

They went to bed. It was Judy's bedroom, which Nicola was sharing as a temporary measure. It had one tiny window offering what Nicola described rather sardonically as 'a magnificent view of the Marylebone

Road'. The bed was a single, with a camp bed beside it. They slept, and when they woke up, Nicola produced a bottle of port she had bought at a fete in the village where she had spent the previous weekend.

'It's not me giving Stacey the stuff, is it?' Carl said. 'It's selling it. That's the problem you've got with it.'

Nicola agreed. 'It wouldn't be so bad if you hadn't sold it. What's Dermot going to do? Or what do you think he's going to do?'

He told her about the rent. The newspapers, maybe the police, Stacey's relatives. 'He calls them "her loved ones".'

They heard the front door close and a set of footsteps on the stairs.

'We'd better get up and go,' Nicola said.

So she was coming home with him. For a moment Carl was almost happy. Out in the street, she asked him again what he thought Dermot was going to do.

'Would it be so bad if he did go to Stacey's relatives, or even the newspapers? You keep saying that giving her the pills wasn't against the law.'

'Having sex with your friend's wife isn't against the law, but you still don't want it known.'

'But let's say you tell Dermot you want the rent and he says OK, you can have it, and the consequence is that he starts telling people – newspapers, police, whatever. Can't you face up to it? The police caution you – isn't that the worst that can happen? You just tell everyone it's not against the law, and in time it'll blow over.'

Carl was silent. Then he said very slowly, 'I know it's not against the law, but the national press – the print media, don't they call it that? – will get hold of it from the *Ham and High* and the *Paddington Express* and they will say exactly what they like about me. I guess the broadsheets like the *Guardian* and the *Independent* may not be that interested – or they may be, but not in a loud screaming headline way. That'll be for the *Sun* and the *Mail*. And they'll run great big headlines in – oh, I don't know, seventy- or eighty-point typeface, and they can do it because all their readers will want to know about an author selling what the paper will call poison to a poor desperate actress who's so overweight people laugh at her.'

'You've really thought about this, haven't you?' said Nicola. 'You've sort of constructed it. Look, let's go and eat somewhere, and forget about this for an evening and a night.'

Very out of character, he threw his arms round her and said loudly so that people stared, 'Oh, Nic, it's so good, it's so lovely to have you back.'

Walking Sybil Soames home from church on Sunday morning was possibly (or 'arguably', as journalists wrote every day in newspapers) the most fateful thing Dermot had ever done in his life. He didn't know this, of course. He didn't arrange it. It happened, that was all.

Sybil shook hands with the vicar and he was the next to do so. They walked down the path from St Mary's, Paddington Green, one after the other and came out together in Venice Walk.

'Are you going my way?' he said.

Because she didn't know what to say, a situation Sybil often found herself in, she blushed and said, 'I don't know.'

'Where do you live?'

'Jerome Crescent. It's sort of Rossmore Road.'

He said no more. He didn't find her attractive. To be attractive, a woman had to look like Angelina Jolie or Caroline the vet: tall, thin as a reed, long-necked, with full lips, dark red hair piled on top of her head. If Dermot had met Sybil Soames anywhere but in church, she might never have become his girlfriend. Sitting next to her by chance in the third pew from the front at St Mary's made speaking to her, and at their fourth meeting asking her out, respectable.

Dermot had very little experience of going out with women, and most of that was with his mother in Skegness, or one of his aunts, who lived next door to his mother. But somehow he could tell that Sybil would not be particular or exacting. She was not good-looking, nor, from the conversation they had had (mostly about the hymns they had sung that morning), particularly intelligent. Perhaps the most attractive thing about her was the admiration she clearly had for him. They talked about the vicar, whose gender Sybil approved of, and Dermot told her he thought women in the clergy was a mistake, while making them bishops was the beginning of the end of Anglicanism in this country.

'Don't you like women, then?' said Sybil.

'Of course I do,' he said. 'In their place.'

He could educate her, he thought. He told her where he worked, making his position at the pet clinic rather more elevated than it was. She seemed to think he must be a vet and he said nothing to correct her. Would she meet him next day for coffee in the Café Rouge in Clifton Road? he wondered. A lot of girls would have asked why not a drink or dinner, but he knew she wouldn't. She was innocent enough to ask him if he was sure he wanted her to meet him.

'I asked you, didn't I?' he said.

'I just wanted to check.'

'One p.m. OK?'

No, she couldn't do that. She'd be at work. She looked almost triumphant, as if she'd known he hadn't meant it.

'OK, make it the evening.'

He didn't care what her work was; she would tell him this when they met. And she was bound to be early, probably ten to seven rather than seven.

He was right. When he arrived at Café Rouge the next evening at five past seven, she was sitting at one of their outside tables. He talked to her about the animal patients at the clinic, describing dog diseases and dog surgery. It turned out that her parents, with whom she lived, had two dogs and she didn't much like them. Animals smelt, she said, and made a mess. She preferred a clean house, and would like one of her own but she'd never afford it. She said this with some passion. He realised he had no need to make another date, but only said he would see her in church on Sunday. Things could go on from there.

'Why don't you grow your hair?' he said. 'It would look a lot better.'

He knew she would. He'd get to work on her clothes next. Maybe persuade her to lose a bit of weight. After all, people were going to see her with him.

Lizzie was going to visit Dermot at the Sutherland Pet Clinic. She remembered Stacey once telling her that her Aunt Yvonne took her cat there for its injections.

She'd also worked out that Gervaise, who'd taken her number but not yet called her, might still be living at home, if he hadn't already gone travelling.

When she had handed over to its parent the last of what the head teacher called 'the kiddiwinks', she got on her bus in the middle bit, which you were not supposed to do because if you were lucky the driver wouldn't see you and you could get away without having a ticket or a pass. This worked very well if you were going no more than two stops. But Lizzie was going a lot further, and the driver was leaning out of his window shaking his fist at her as she tripped lightly down Sutherland Avenue.

Dermot was happy to talk to her when he learned that she knew Carl and had been one of Stacey's closest friends. He told her about Stacey's aunt, Mrs Weatherspoon, whose son and daughter both lived with her in her mansion at Swiss Cottage.

'Poor Stacey left her apartment in Primrose Hill to her aunt, as I expect you know. I shouldn't say it, but it doesn't seem quite fair, does it? "To him that hath shall be given and from him that hath not everything shall be taken away, even that which he hath."'

'Is that right?' Lizzie had no idea what he meant, and didn't care. 'You know, Stacey once gave me her aunt's phone number, but I've mislaid it. Would you let me have it?'

'I couldn't do that,' said Dermot in unctuous tones. 'But I could give her yours and ask her to call you.'

She's already got it, or her son has, thought Lizzie. It

was a piece of luck that at that moment the vet called out to Dermot to come and give her a hand with Dusky. 'Excuse me,' said Dermot.

By another piece of luck, he had also left Yvonne Weatherspoon's details on the computer. Lizzie, popping behind the counter, committed landline and mobile numbers to her excellent memory, then, on the principle of better safe than sorry, exited the file and quickly afterwards the clinic.

Back in Kilburn by six, a good time to phone anyone, Lizzie was soon speaking to Gervaise Weatherspoon, who happened to answer his mother's phone.

'I'm so glad to have caught you,' she said. 'I was hoping we might have a talk before you go on your trip. About the apartment in Pinetree Court, I mean.'

'Oh yes?'

'It's just an idea I had. I don't want to talk about it on the phone.'

He sounded strangely hostile. 'Where did you want to talk about it then?'

'I thought perhaps in the apartment?'

'OK. Tomorrow morning? Ten a.m.? I'll be there.'

The first time Lizzie had seen Gervaise, she had been dressed in jeans and a sweatshirt. The idea today would be to create a glamorous image, so she put on the green suit she had worn for that evening visit to her parents. Getting on the bus in Kilburn High Road, she presented her pass this time and settled into her seat, conscious that she was the best-dressed woman there. Not that there was much competition from this bunch, who looked as if they were all off to clean out someone's drains.

She was five minutes late, but Gervaise wasn't there. Irritated, she waited outside Stacey's front door and wondered what she would do if he didn't come. But he did, arriving just as she was making her contingency plans and letting them both in.

Inside, he looked her up and down. 'That thing you're wearing looks exactly like one Stacey had in her slimmer days.'

'Does it? Well, it isn't hers. Stacey was never as thin as me.'

He laughed. 'Don't you girls ever watch films from the fifties? All the women in them are what you call fat. Marilyn Monroe was a size sixteen.'

Lizzie didn't say anything. She wondered what he was trying to prove. 'When are you going to wherever it is? Thailand, was it?'

He seemed to find that funny too. 'Cambodia and Laos. Next week. Why?'

'Well, I thought you might want someone to look after the place while you're away. I mean, live here, keep it clean. I wouldn't want paying.'

His apparently irrepressible laughter was bubbling up again. 'I don't suppose you would,' he said. 'I don't suppose you'd want to pay me either.' He made no answer to her offer, but strolled into the bedroom. Lizzie followed him. He opened the wardrobe doors and peered inside. She was conscious once again of how good-looking he was. 'I wonder what happened to Stacey's clothes. There's not much here.'

Apart from the green suit and a few other items, they were all in Lizzie's cupboards in Kilburn. She had an answer for him. 'Someone must have taken them to that designer seconds shop in Lauderdale Road.'

'Ah,' he said. 'Of course.' He looked at his watch. No one else of his age that Lizzie knew had a watch. They all told the time on their mobiles or iPads. 'I have an appointment in St James's in half an hour, so I'm afraid we must terminate this interview. It's been delightful.'

Lizzie had lost all her confidence and now felt very small and inferior, but she had not entirely lost her nerve. 'Well, can I stay here while you're away?'

'Oh, didn't I say? Of course you can. We'll keep in touch while I'm in Cambodia.' There was no invitation to have a drink or even dinner before he left; no laughter this time, only a broad smile. 'I won't need to give you a key, I'm sure you've got one already.'

She nodded in stupefied silence.

'I'll leave you a phone number.'

Would you be able to call a mobile number in Cambodia? Lizzie wondered. Gervaise produced a receipt from his pocket, and wrote in pencil on the back of it what was obviously a landline number. She put it in her handbag.

Once he had gone, and she had helped herself to a long draught of tequila for what her grandmother would have called medicinal purposes, she made a survey of the flat. Since Gervaise hadn't checked what was in the place apart from the absence of clothes, she would be able to help herself to whatever she wanted. The days of getting into people's flats or houses and taking some small item away with her seemed long past.

The bathroom was still crowded with make-up and perfume, most of it barely used. She would have all that. The Roberts radio wouldn't be missed, she thought, and nor would the nearly-new camera. Was there anything in the flat she could sell? Maybe what her mother quaintly called cutlery? But no. She had never stooped to stealing and she mustn't start now.

After another swig of tequila, she went downstairs to tell the concierge that she was looking after the flat for the next – how long? She didn't know; say, eight weeks? But Gervaise had already given him the news, and it seemed not to have gone down well. The man scowled behind the black-framed sunglasses he wore, which seemed a strange choice as it had come on to rain and the sky was very dark.

CHAPTER THIRTEEN

It was a little late in the day to take a bus to Hampstead Heath, Tom Milsom thought, but now that it was light for sixteen hours of the day, he hadn't really noticed it was nearly five when he left home. Still, his favourite bus, the number 6, had taken him to the stop outside the Tesco in Clifton Road and the flower shop, and there he got on the single-decker 46, which took him to Fitzjohn's Avenue.

The houses up here were huge four-storey places, most of them sheltered and veiled by tall creeper-hung trees. Tom wondered if just one family or even a couple lived in them, or were they divided into flats? 'Flats' wasn't a suitable word. You would have to call them 'apartments' and the houses 'mansions'. Although quite heavy traffic filled the road, the whole area was oddly silent. Few people were about, and no young ones. Tom saw a youngish woman in very high heels taking a dog out for its walk, a dog you couldn't mistake for a mongrel or a cross-breed, it was so unmistakably pedigree, with its slender, elegant shape, sleek cream-coloured fur and legs rather like its owner's. The collar it wore was black leather studded with green and blue jewels.

This was a safe, quiet bus, his fellow passengers mostly middle-aged and elderly women, all middle class and with shopping bags. Working women would have shrieked, or at any rate gasped, when the bus driver had to stamp on his brakes and judder to a stop as a teenager in a long scarlet sports car charged across Nutley Terrace right in front of him, yet these women barely reacted. Tom got out by Hampstead station, which he remembered was the deepest below ground in the London Underground system – or was that Highgate? Hampstead was very pretty. That was a word a man should never use, he thought as he walked down Rosslyn Hill, except perhaps about a girl. A thin drizzle was falling.

Should he try and find the house where Keats had lived? There seemed very little point when all he knew about Keats was a poem about a knight-at-arms and a woman who had no mercy that he had had to learn at school. Anyway, he didn't know whether the house was in Downshire Hill or in Keats Grove, where it ought to be, and he didn't want to show his ignorance by asking. He could have some tea instead. Perhaps he ought to buy something, a little present for Dorothy, and what better place than Hampstead? It was a bit ridiculous, for he was hardly on holiday, but he bought it just the same, a book of notelets, one for every day of the year, with 'Hampstead Queen of the Hills' printed on it in Gothic lettering. He had a cup of tea and a millionaire's macaroon before going off to find the bus home.

The kind of people who made trouble on buses were not to be found in Hampstead. The Hampstead sort all had valid passes, plenty of silver coins should the pass mysteriously have become obsolete, and a driving licence for ID. Tom had all this, and the bus he was getting on was the prestigious 24 that plied between Hampstead Heath and Victoria, taking in Camden Town and Westminster on its way.

He got on and sat in a small single seat tucked away behind the driver's cab. The girl who followed him, instead of touching her pass to the reader as he had done, turned away and got on halfway down, after Tom's daughter's fashion. He waited for her to go up to the driver and either present her pass or put down the requisite two pounds forty. Neither happened. Should he approach the driver himself and tell him? Or hand the girl the coins, which he happened to have? But she was on her phone, talking to someone with whom she appeared on intimate terms.

Tom felt indignant. How dare she impose on what the government called 'the hard-working taxpayer' and have a free ride? Walking up the bus, he said, 'Excuse me' into the driver's window. The entire lower floor of the bus had stopped talking and was paying him close attention. He dropped his voice to a whisper. The driver said the girl probably hadn't got a pass or any spare money. He seemed displeased, not grateful and friendly as Tom felt he should have been. Wondering if this would produce a warmer response, Tom laid down the two-pound coin and the two twenties.

'What's that for?' said the driver. 'Her? Cash payments stopped last month. By law.'

The girl was still on her mobile, talking in a rather indignant way, and when the driver pulled the bus in to the kerb and stopped, Tom began to feel nervous. Whatever happened next, he would be drawn into it. Standing up, he watched the doors at the front of the bus come open, muttered, 'Got to get off,' and jumped out on to the pavement. He looked back over his shoulder. The driver and the girl appeared to be in a fierce argument as he walked away down the hill.

Tom wasn't sure what to do. It was a long walk from here to Willesden, and bad enough to the number 6 route. He didn't even know which way the number 6 went between Clifton Road and Willesden Green. Perhaps he should make for the Beatles' place in what-was-it, Abbey Road. The bus he had got off passed him, sending spray up from the water in the gutter. It wasn't exactly dark yet, but getting that way.

He was almost at the next bus stop by now. The best thing would be to wait there, as by now he had no idea where he was. People were waiting for the next 24: two young men, no more than boys. One of them said to him, 'Got a ciggie, Grandad?'

Tom wanted to ask him how he dared call him that, but he was frightened. 'I don't smoke,' he muttered.

The other one said, 'Don't you lie to me,' and grabbed him by the shoulders, shaking him.

Tom made a whimpering sound. He was released so violently that he staggered. The one who had asked him for a cigarette pushed himself in front of him and punched him hard in the stomach, a blow powerful enough to knock him over. He fell to the ground, doubled up. The two men kicked him on to a patch of grass under a tree and, as the 24 bus came, ran away.

I n Falcon Mews, something crashed on to the floor from the flat above. It must have been heavy, a saucepan or a bucket. The sound it made reverberated through the house, followed by footsteps running down the stairs and the front door slamming.

The noise went on like this every day, only stopping when Dermot went to work. Carl knew it must be deliberate, intended to annoy him. It had started about the time the August rent was due but of course never came. The noise varied: a crash made by something dropped, doors slamming, the piercing growl of an electric drill, the hammering of a nail into the wall, the TV on full, the radio playing hymns and all the doors up there wide open.

The houses in Falcon Mews were Victorian jerry-built with thin walls and not very substantial floors, so that every sound echoed and trembled. When the noise first began, Carl had been irritated by it. Now it had started to frighten him. Could the neighbours hear it, the Pembrokes on the left side, Elinor Jackson on the right? They hadn't complained to him, but then he hadn't complained to Dermot either. He and Dermot barely spoke to each other any more. Dermot no longer knocked on one of the doors in his part of the house to make some fatuous remark. Instead he ran faster than ever down the stairs and burst out into the street, banging the front door behind him.

While Nicola was at home, the noise stopped altogether. This behaviour on Dermot's part was so transparent, so obvious, that Carl found it almost incredible. Now, if he told her his tenant made a deliberate racket simply to annoy him, she wouldn't believe it. He had told her, though, and she had begun to treat him as if he was imagining the bangs and crashes and might be hearing things as a result of the nervous state he had worked himself up into.

'I've got a couple of weeks' holiday owing to me,' she said. 'Why shouldn't we go away somewhere? It would be good for you.'

'I can't afford it. Well, I can now, but I soon won't be able to if I don't get any rent.'

That only led to her giving him the advice she always gave him. 'Tell him you must have the rent and let him . . . well, do his worst. No one can charge you with anything. You won't go to prison. Tell him to go ahead and talk to these people and the newspapers, and once you've done it you'll feel a great relief and we'll go to Cornwall or Guernsey or somewhere.'

Dermot was out. The house was silent. It was Sunday, so he was probably in church, but he would soon be back and the noise would start again.

'I can't,' he said. 'I mean that literally. I can't do it. I can't allow him to shame me. And yet it's such a little thing, isn't it? Sometimes I dream he's dead, and when

I wake up and he's not . . . I lie there and hear him drop something, or his telly comes on, and I know he's alive and there's nothing I can do.'

Nicola was looking at him in horror. 'Oh, Carl, sweetheart.'

The front door opened and closed softly and Dermot's footsteps tiptoed up the stairs. Carl put his head in his hands.

'Let's hope this has taught you that riding around to dodgy places on buses isn't a good idea,' said Dot Milsom.

'Oh, Mum, Hampstead's not a dodgy place.' Lizzie was more shocked by this description of London's loveliest suburb than by her father's experience.

'On your own, too,' said Dot. 'I did offer to come with you, you'll remember.'

'You're not old enough.' Tom laughed at his own wit. 'It's not the kind of thing that happens more than once, anyway. It looks to me like the girl I reported to the bus driver phoned her boyfriend, and it was him waiting to clobber me.'

A passer-by had found him struggling to get up and called an ambulance, which took him to St Mary's Hospital, where he was treated for various cuts and bruises. It was discovered that no ribs were broken, but he was kept in overnight and allowed home next morning. For now he could just about walk with someone holding his arm.

Lizzie had come with her mother to see him in hospital and had told her parents in great detail about what she called her new job, looking after her friend Stacey's state-of-the-art apartment in Primrose Hill. Tom again thought about his daughter's flat in Kilburn. But his thoughts were mostly on his recent ordeal. The breezy attitude he adopted as he recounted his encounter with the two young men, and that he continued with the police officer who called to ask him what had happened, was a show of bravado and not what he really felt.

Of course, some would say it was his own fault, provoking that girl by shopping her to the driver. But wasn't that the duty of a good citizen? I wouldn't do it again, though, he thought. I'd lie low. But even making this resolve failed to give him confidence. He postponed the idea of getting on the number 82 bus, which had been his next project. Instead, now that his bruises were getting better, his headache from hitting his head when they kicked him over gone, he planned to take himself up to Edgware or Harrow at the end of the week.

But when Thursday came – Friday was the day planned for this excursion – he went to bed dreading the next morning and found it impossible to sleep. He lay awake tossing and turning and only fell asleep at five a.m., to be jerked awake by a dream, not about an assault in Haverstock Hill but a car crash in Willesden Lane.

At breakfast, he told Dorothy he wouldn't be taking a bus ride that day. 'Very wise,' she said. 'You can come with me to have a look at Lizzie's lovely apartment.'

CHAPTER FOURTEEN

Elizabeth Holbrook had divorced her husband after fifteen months of marriage and was now living in her mother's house.

'I suppose you'll revert to your maiden name,' said Yvonne Weatherspoon.

'How ridiculous is that? Maiden name indeed. Anyway, I won't. I always hated being called Weatherspoon. I more or less got married to get Leo's name.'

'It's nice to have you back,' said her mother insincerely. 'You're not thinking of moving into a place of your own?'

'If that was what you wanted, you might have given Stacey's flat to me instead of Gervaise.'

In fact, Elizabeth had no real quarrel with the way things had turned out. Her mother had five bedrooms, a self-contained flat in the basement, a cleaner every morning and two cars. The only drawback to the house in Swiss Cottage was that cat. Elizabeth had attempted in the past to show Sophie who was boss, but never stood a chance. Their first – and almost their last – encounter had been when Elizabeth had roughly removed her from the seat of an armchair, and Sophie had turned on her, teeth bared, claws out, and inflicted some nasty wounds before returning to her favourite spot. These days they gave each other a wide berth.

Days passed and no rent had appeared. Carl hadn't expected it, but he was still angry and miserable. He also knew that Dermot was playing some sort of complicated game, for after a week or two, the noise had stopped. Even the front door was closed silently. It was so quiet that there might have been no tenant on the top floor if he had not occasionally seen Dermot walking down Falcon Mews, on his way to or from work or leaving for church. Then, in the middle of the next week, something made of metal – a watering can, perhaps – was dropped, and crashed resoundingly, bouncing across the floor above. Because he was no longer used to it and had believed the noise had come to an end, Carl shivered and actually cried out.

There was no more noise that day, but it left him trembling. Nicola was due home at six thirty, but he couldn't bear to wait that long, not so much because he wanted her company as out of terror that the dropping of things was due to start again.

When he phoned her, she said she had the afternoon off and would come home in an hour's time. Having her here would be wonderful, were it not for the fact that she would constantly urge him to stand up to Dermot and demand the rent. But he had to have her here for this coming weekend. He couldn't live without her. He had done no work for weeks now. The book was a dead loss, not a book at all in fact, for he had destroyed all of it, even the plan and the notes he had made before he started. He had never wanted a real job, but now he wished he had one. It would get him out of the house. He read in the paper and saw on the television that jobs were very hard to get. It was hopeless for him even to look for employment.

On Friday afternoon, on his way back to work, Dermot knocked on Carl's living room door. Carl was asleep. He got off the sofa and opened the door.

'Yes, what is it?'

'Just to ask you if it'd be all right to use the garden sometimes, sit out there, I mean. I've got a couple of deckchairs.'

Carl said, 'That would mean coming through my kitchen.'

'That's right. OK with you?' Implicit in the enquiry was *it had better be.* '"A garden is a lovesome thing, God wot",' said Dermot.

Carl shrugged, nodded, shut the door. He wondered why he ever spoke politely to Dermot. Why even answer him? Silence would be best, but he knew he wouldn't keep silent. Was it because he clung to some hopeless hope that Dermot would relent, that he would say he hadn't meant it, it was a try-on, and now, soon, he would pay the rent as he had always known he must?

When Nicola came in from work, Carl was waiting for her, sitting on the front step, maybe just to escape from breathing the same air as Dermot. Money was short. The lack of it was beginning to make itself felt in a serious way, and this was something Carl couldn't admit to Nicola. Even though he had grown up in a world where women were becoming increasingly equal to men, where equality was the subject of almost daily TV programmes and constant newspaper features, he had still absorbed enough of a male supremacy culture to believe that, if he were to mention his financial crisis, Nicola would think he was asking her for a loan or even a gift. And she would press him again to confront his tenant.

On Sunday, they watched from a window as Dermot went to church. Like churchgoers in times gone by, he carried a prayer book. They had talked about Dermot for half the night, what he would do if crossed, and what the consequences would be. They did make love, at just before three, and afterwards fell into a heavy sleep until nearly ten. Saturday's rain had stopped during the night. The sun was out, the wind had dropped and Mr Kaleejah was taking his dog for its morning walk. It always walked along in a docile way, pausing sometimes to look up at Mr Kaleejah and wag its tail. Carl had never heard it bark.

'He'll bring his deckchairs through the kitchen to the back door,' said Carl. 'Why deckchairs? One for him, and who's the other for? Perhaps he's got friends, but I've never seen them. The next thing will be he'll want to take over one of my rooms. He's got a living room, a kitchen, a bathroom and a bedroom. Maybe he wants another bedroom? He could take over my second bedroom. Why not? I can't stop him.'

'Yes, you can, Carl. He can tell his story to anyone he likes. How do you know they'll even care? They'll probably say, so what? If they're even interested, they'll google it and see that what you did wasn't against the law. Tell him you want the rent and if he says no you'll evict him. That's what anyone else would do.'

She made it sound so simple, Carl thought. He watched Dermot turn the corner into Castellain Road and disappear. He put his head in his hands, a frequent gesture with him these days.

The day continued fine, becoming sunnier and warmer. 'Let's go out for lunch,' said Nicola in a cheerful tone, though she felt anything but cheerful.

'I can't afford it.'

'Well, I can. You'll have to face up to that, Carl. When you do what I suggest, you'll have some money and you'll feel much better because things won't be as bad as you think. Probably they won't be bad at all. Come on, we'll go out, and we won't be here to see Dermot come back.'

So they went round to the Café Rouge, ate fishcakes and chips and lemon tart and drank a lot of red wine. 'You'll think I'm crazy,' said Carl, 'but I don't want to go back there. I can't bear to be under the same roof as him.'

'I live there too, you know. When you tell him to do his worst, I'll be with you. We'll confront him together.'

The sun was very hot and the house warm and stuffy

when they got home. Nicola went upstairs and looked out of the bedroom window. She called Carl. 'You're not going to like this, but you'd better see it.'

No one had attended to the garden since Carl's father had died; in fact since long before that. Where the lawn had been, the grass had grown tall and turned to hay, and the flower beds were dense with stinging nettles three feet tall. Two deckchairs covered in red-and-blue-striped canvas had been put up among the hay, and in them sat Dermot and a rather large young woman with shaggy dark hair wearing a dirndl skirt and peasant blouse. Carl made a sound like a howl of agony.

'Who's that woman?'

'His girlfriend, I should think.'

'He hasn't got a girlfriend.'

'Well, he has now.'

A visit from her parents was not to be welcomed by Lizzie. Usually, that was. Now, however, in possession of Stacey's beautiful flat, she felt very different. Not just on account of the decor and furnishings, but because quite a lot of exotic drink still remained from Stacey's store, as well as tins of the sort of biscuits and snacks that went well with drink.

Tom and Dot had been in the flat no more than ten minutes, had examined the large refrigerator, the freezer and the washing machine and drier as well as the living room and bedroom furnishings and the two flat-screen televisions, when they were plied with dry Oloroso and

Tequila Sunrises. Conversation concentrated on Tom's recovery from his assault on Haverstock Hill. Lizzie, who didn't take admonition well herself, told him how careful he must be in future, and to be sure to take his mobile with him and phone her or her mother at the least sign of danger. Dot agreed, but added that it was useless to say anything as Tom never did what he was told.

Advice, in any case, was unnecessary. They both thought privately that Tom had given up his exploration of London on buses. It had, in their opinion, been ridiculous, and fortunately, and without too much harm being done, had been ended by the Haverstock Hill attack. Both Dot and Lizzie were now putting their minds to some alternative hobby for him and already had ideas: golf, for instance, though Willesden was a long way from a golf course; the Willesden cycling club, though Tom didn't possess a bicycle, and anyway, look how many cyclists got knocked down by lorries; dog-walking, which considering they had no dog was never taken seriously. None of these options was mentioned to Tom.

U p to now, Tom Milsom had led a calm, steady, peaceable life. His job had been largely trouble-free. His wife loved and respected him, or seemed to. His daughter – well, she took his money, he thought bitterly, and for a flat she no longer even lived in. What did they think of him, the pair of them, for giving up an interest he had plainly enjoyed because two boys had hit him? Part of him never wanted to get on a bus again, even though it was not the buses' fault. In fact he had not even been *on* a bus when the boys had attacked him. This line of reasoning sent him out of the house – though perhaps it was more the result of Dorothy plying the vacuum cleaner round the armchair he was sitting in.

He walked about a mile, thinking it was good for him, then got on the number 139 bus. It was only then that it occurred to him he should have looked at London Bus Routes online. Perhaps when he got to Baker Street he could find a number 1. There was something fascinating, intriguing, about a bus numbered 1. It ought to be the best of all London buses. He asked the driver, who told him to stay on till Waterloo and pick up the number 1 there, which would take him to Bermondsey and Canada Water. Relaxing in the back of the 139 once more – there were several empty seats – Tom felt enormously better. He had always wondered what Canada Water was like, what Canada Water *was,* and now he would find out.

The sun was shining; it would be light for hours. Nothing was going to happen today or on the days to come. The trouble with those two boys had been no more than a nasty incident. Luckily he hadn't been much hurt and all was going to be well.

CHAPTER FIFTEEN

Nicola wanted to protect Carl from Dermot, but she didn't tell Carl this. No matter how far emancipation had progressed towards equality, a woman might tell a man she wanted to care for him but she could not admit to him that she wanted to defend him from another man. Anyway, she seldom saw Dermot. If she heard him on the stairs, she kept inside the living room until the front door closed. They had met only once recently, in the hallway, she going out and he coming in, he from the pet clinic and carrying shopping, she on her way to buy something for an evening meal.

'You're living here full time again now, are you?' he had asked. There were several ways of putting that enquiry, and Dermot's phrasing was rather accusatory, the implication being that she shouldn't have been. She would have liked to ask him if he had any objection, but Carl's fear of Dermot was beginning to affect her too.

'I am, yes,' she said.

He shook his head, the kind of gesture that implied

wonder more than disapproval. 'As I always say,' he said, 'it takes all sorts to make a world.'

She said nothing about it to Carl. When she got back with the two ready meals and a bottle of rosé, her anger, which was considerable, had died down. Dermot was upstairs but silent apart from a burst of 'Amazing Grace' when he briefly opened his front door.

Next day was Saturday, the weather improved, and he was out in the garden with the two deckchairs, though only one was occupied. He must have sneaked – as Carl put it – through the kitchen with them while Carl and Nicola were out.

'You'll have to tell him you don't want him in the garden,' said Nicola. They were in the bedroom, looking down on the top of Dermot's head.

Carl didn't say anything.

'You'll have to, Carl. This is only the thin end of the wedge.'

'I've already told him he can use the garden.'

'Don't you think that if he was going to tell anyone – I mean about selling that stuff to Stacey—'

'I know what you mean. I think about it every day. It haunts me. I know what you were going to say. That if he was going to tell the newspapers or her aunt or her cousins or *anyone*, he'd have done it by now. But why would he? He has the perfect arrangement. He could tell them tomorrow or next week. It's not something that gets easier for me, is it? The newspapers will send someone around here to interview me. He's biding his time, as he might say. He's waiting for someone or something to trigger it, and me telling him he can't sit out in my garden might be just the trigger he needs.'

The weather went on being nice, and Dermot sat out in the garden again the next day. Carl and Nicola knew he would, because he left the deckchairs out overnight. This, Carl said, was the thickening end of the wedge, or was it the further thinning? Dermot had gone to church, of course, carrying his Alternative Service book. Carl, like many atheists, disapproved of that work, preferring the Book of Common Prayer, and would have liked to say so scathingly to Dermot but was afraid. His tenant – could you describe someone as a tenant when they paid no rent? – returned at eleven thirty with the fat dark girl. They sat in the garden for an hour, then the deckchairs were vacated and soon a strong smell of curry permeated the house.

Carl and Nicola went out. They had a drink in the Prince Alfred around the corner. It was a fine old pub, much loved by Nicola and once loved by Carl. He loved it no longer; there was nothing that he loved.

'Except you,' he said. 'I love you a lot. I really love you, but how can I marry you?' He had never mentioned marriage before. 'This torment will go on for ever, for the rest of my life. I know it sounds mad, but it's true. I shall live in this house or another house and he will be there with me, wherever it is. He will never go and I can't get rid of him. Sometimes I think I'll kill myself.'

*

Weeks had passed since Yvonne Weatherspoon had been to the pet clinic. Sophie was well and no injections were due, but a new event in the Weatherspoon household had taken place. Elizabeth had occasionally opened the French windows for the cat to go out in the evenings, and Sophie had stayed out until dawn, squealing under Yvonne's bedroom window to be let in. This truancy had badly frightened Yvonne, and she was even more distressed when she saw that Sophie had a wound on her neck and a triangle of furry skin nipped from one of her ears. She had plainly been fighting with the Bengal next door.

'This is what happens when you have your children home to live,' Yvonne told Dermot the next morning, referring of course to Elizabeth, not Sophie.

'You wouldn't be without her,' said Dermot in a sentimental tone.

'There's no question of that. Will Caroline be able to see me? Well, see *her*, poor darling.'

'I expect we can fit you in. Sophie will have to have intravenous antibiotics.' Dermot liked to display medical knowledge picked up from Caroline, Darren and Melissa without actually knowing anything about it.

'I should have phoned first. I know that.' Yvonne brought her face very close to his across the desktop. 'But you see, if I did that, I thought you'd say no, maybe say there was no room for us.'

'Not this time.' Dermot smiled his toothy yellow smile. 'Now here's Melissa come for you. I'm afraid Caroline's out on a call.'

Left alone, and with no other pet-owners due until the afternoon, he let his mind wander on to Stacey Warren and the pills that Carl had given – no, sold – her. He mustn't tell, he knew that beyond a doubt. It would be different if Carl had demanded the rent and threatened eviction, but it was unlikely that he would do that as he was too frightened.

No one had ever been afraid of Dermot before, or not to this degree, and it gratified him to have caused someone this amount of fear without violence or even the threat of it. A shame really that he couldn't have it both ways: not tell Stacey's aunt or cousins, say not a word to the *Ham & High*, but drop a hint just the same to Carl as to how near to danger he had come and would come again. Of course the game would have to end at some point. He had no intention of being evicted. He would have to quietly resume paying rent. But not now. Not for a long time. For now he would keep the money, keep the fear up, and keep Carl exactly where he wanted him.

Yvonne came back into reception with Sophie wearing a wide white collar designed to prevent her claws from tearing at her wound. In this purpose it was already failing.

'I shall have to have a taxi back,' said Yvonne. 'I had to have one here. I couldn't have Sophie with me loose in the car.'

Dermot would have told her it was against the law anyway, but he had told her that on numerous previous occasions. He called a taxi for her. 'It'll be up to fifteen minutes.'

This was an opportunity too perfect to ignore. True, Sophie was whimpering, but this place reverberated and echoed to the cries and growls of animals. Yvonne was sitting down now, murmuring soft words to the cat. 'You must be missing your niece, Mrs Weatherspoon.' Dermot broached the subject with extreme politeness.

Yvonne looked surprised. 'Yes, well, of course. It was very sad.'

'Indeed it was. More than that. Tragic really. Drugs are everywhere these days, aren't they?'

The cat, satisfied that the torture was over and might not recur, had fallen asleep. Yvonne sighed, shook her head. 'I'm glad to say neither of my children ever took them.'

Dermot didn't believe her. 'You're lucky,' he said, seeing the taxi arrive. 'It's worse, I would think, when someone one trusts – a so-called friend – gives or even sells such horrible substances to one's loved one.'

The seed was planted. Yvonne smiled vaguely, said he was right and allowed him to carry cat and cat box out on to the pavement. She would remember what he had said, he thought, but he had given nothing away. If things continued as they were, he need reveal no more.

Meanwhile, Sybil had become quite a useful tool. She liked sitting in the garden, as her parents had nothing like it in Jerome Crescent. From what he gathered, there was nothing much in Jerome Crescent that Sybil liked. The previous Sunday, as they'd walked back together to Falcon Mews, she'd asked him if she could do some weeding. She put her request humbly and with a lot of excuses because she was afraid of offending him.

'Good idea,' he said.

'You won't have to ask Mr Martin, will you?' She always called Carl Mr Martin.

'Good gracious, no. We're the best of pals. He'll be grateful.'

So while Dermot slumbered gently in his deckchair the following Sunday afternoon, placing the *Observer* open on his face to protect it from the sun just as his grandfather used to do, Sybil pulled up nettles, campions and docks and dug out their roots with a trowel.

From the bedroom window, Carl looked down on them. Getting your garden weeded wasn't exactly something you could object to. But surely they could have asked? Besides, taking what Dermot would undoubtedly call a liberty would just lead to another. First the deckchairs; now that girl was digging up his garden. What would be next? He had suggested to Nicola that Dermot's next move would be to take over one of Carl's own rooms. No doubt that would soon happen.

But something else did. Not a takeover, but an inter-ference in his personal life.

'Been wining and dining, have you?' Carl and Nicola had just come in from dinner in Camden with Carl's mother, Una.

Carl didn't reply. He expected Dermot to go upstairs, but his tenant said, 'Could I come in for a minute? I've got something I want to say to you.'

Taking over the second bedroom, Carl thought, that

was what it would be. He opened the living room door and Nicola went through to the kitchen. 'These things are always awkward, aren't they?' Dermot smiled with his lips closed. 'But I'm not easily embarrassed.'

'What did you want to say?'

Nicola had come back into the room. She had a glass of water in her hand.

'Well, it's unfortunate, but it's something that must be said. You were living alone when I first came here, Carl, but now you're living with this – this young lady. Miss Townsend. This isn't right. It is in fact far from right. I'm not old-fashioned, I'm a progressive kind of cove, but there I draw the line. I don't call it living in sin, that would be to go too far, but it is – to put it plainly – wrong. Now I'm sure you'll agree with me when you think about it.'

Nicola drank the water, all of it down at one gulp. She said afterwards that now she knew the meaning of 'stupefied'.

'How about you living with that woman you bring to the house? That's different, is it?' Carl asked.

'Ah, very different, Carl. We don't live together, you see. I have just come back from taking Sybil home to her parents in Jerome Crescent.' Dermot nodded sagely. 'Well, I've said my piece, got it off my chest, and I suggest that when you think about it, you'll find I'm right.'

CHAPTER SIXTEEN

'Where's Jerome Crescent?'

It was three fifteen in the morning and Carl hadn't slept at all. Nicola was fast asleep, but she woke up when he asked the question a second time and even more loudly.

She turned over in bed. 'What?'

'That woman Sybil lives there.'

'Carl, I have to go to work in the morning.'

'I don't know why I'm asking,' he said. 'It doesn't matter. Go back to sleep.'

He thought he would never sleep again. He lay there for a little while, maybe ten minutes, and then got up and went down to the kitchen. The house was as silent as if it had been a cottage in a country lane.

Upstairs, two floors up, Dermot would be asleep, deeply asleep in bed, without worries, at peace. He probably drank cocoa or Ovaltine at bedtime, and the mug it had been in would be on his bedside table. There would be a bin for the washing in his room, and before he went to bed he would drop his clothes in it. Things would be like that every night, night after night, unchanging, on and on, while he, Carl, wandered wakeful around the house, growing poorer and poorer, eventually going on the dole or benefits or whatever it was called. For him things would never change, but they would change for Dermot, who would marry that Sybil and have children with her. He'd get a better job, flourish, and one day seek him out, and he, Carl, would be a wretched broken creature in rags, in a shabby, dirty room, and Dermot would offer to buy the house from him. Offer him half the price the other houses in Falcon Mews fetched because he could . . .

You must stop this, he told himself, you will drive yourself mad. But what did you do when you were caught in a trap as he was? You had to decide which was worse (or better): to be utterly disgraced, your name all over the papers, your writing career ruined, to be interviewed and photographed as the man who sold poison to an unsuspecting young girl and brought about her death; or to escape that by giving up all you possessed, your only means of making a living. He couldn't see a way out. It was one or the other.

He went into the living room, took a bottle of gin, the only spirits he had, and swigged what remained of it, about a glassful. As he swallowed it, he thought, I am mad, I am crazy, I shall be ill, and he lay down on Dad's sofa, staring at the ceiling and breathing like someone who had run a race. If he ever had another book published and it was ever reviewed, the journalist would refer to him as 'the disgraced author Carl Martin'.

The gin had its effect, swinging the room around, deadening him, knocking him unconscious. Nicola found him four hours later and lay down beside him, holding him in her arms.

Old Albert Weatherspoon, who had been Elizabeth and Gervaise's grandfather, used to say that two women could never share a kitchen. It was just one of his many misogynistic maxims, and Elizabeth would have been the first to rise up in wrath at such an instance of sexism, along with his other sayings, such as that women made bad drivers. But having lived at home with her mother for a couple of months, she was ready to admit that two women could never share a house.

'If you'd known that Gervaise wasn't going to live in Pinetree Court but was going to announce plans to go off to Cambodia, would you have given the flat to me instead of him?'

'You'd got a home and a husband. How was I to know that you and Leo would split up? There was no warning.'

'How could there be a warning? When you're in a relationship, you don't tell everyone that although things are all right now, they may go wrong in a couple of months' time, do you?'

'I don't know. I haven't lived like you do, jumping about from one man to another.'

'I can't stay here, I do know that,' said Elizabeth. 'We have a row every day. And as for that cat, I'd drown it if I could get near it without being torn to pieces.'

'Don't you lay a finger on my sweet lamb.' Yvonne stood up, quivering. 'You can do as you like with the flat. I don't want it. But I don't want any trouble. Remember that.' She considered for a moment. 'I'd be quite pleased if you could get rid of that Lizzie woman. Milsom, she's called. I know she was a friend of Stacey, but it can't be right that she's still living there. It was your brother who told her she could. Amazing what a pretty face can do, isn't it?'

'Pretty?' said Elizabeth. 'I don't think so.'

Yvonne was almost as anxious to get rid of Elizabeth as Elizabeth was to move. Although Sophie was obviously capable of defending herself, Yvonne was afraid her daughter might find a way of doing her real harm. Both Elizabeth and Sophie were free to wander about the house at night, and Yvonne began having bad dreams of her daughter putting poison in the cat's dish.

So Yvonne went to Pinetree Court to speak to the concierge. He knew who she was, and would have much preferred her as the occupant of the flat. As far as he was concerned, she was the owner of what he called 'the property', and the sooner she moved in, the better. Yvonne could understand this. A handsome, obviously wealthy woman in the prime of life – she would never call herself middle-aged – was a more suitable occupant than a twenty-four-year-old. That it would actually be her daughter who would be living there wasn't his business, she thought. She would like the lock changed – could he arrange that? Of course she understood that changing the locks on the entrance to the whole block would not be possible.

'I'll do what I can,' said the concierge. 'It may take a few days.'

Mrs Weatherspoon phoned Lizzie and asked her to vacate the flat on the following day, as her daughter would be moving in and the lock would be changed. Lizzie put up a weak defence that she was here at Gervaise's invitation, and Yvonne told her not to be silly. It was five in the afternoon and Lizzie had just returned from playschool. She poured herself a large vodka and orange – the first of a new bottle – and decided that there was nothing for it but to get out the next day.

Swithin Campbell, her phone said, ringing musically. 'Come out with me tonight, Liz?' he said. 'I'll call for you at seven.'

It gave her very little time to get ready, but five minutes would have been enough. She rushed into the bedroom and got into a bright red bra and pants and Stacey's black dress with the white lace panel down the front. Jo Malone's Pomegranate Noir was sprayed down her cleavage. She slid her feet into Stacey's most uncomfortable shoes, the red ones with the four-inch heels. By the time she was sitting down again, finishing off the vodka, the doorbell was ringing.

It wasn't Swithin. The man at the door told Lizzie

he was Mr Newman's driver, sent to fetch her. Mr Newman was waiting outside in the car.

Swithin wasn't called Newman but Campbell, but Lizzie didn't think this important. Newman was probably his business partner or something.

He stepped inside, and Lizzie felt something rammed into her spine and let out a shriek that there was no one around to hear. He showed her the gun, then replaced it on her spine and said, 'We're going to walk downstairs, you first.'

Of course she did, trembling by now. The gun wasn't real. It was a toy that the driver had borrowed from his five-year-old nephew, but Lizzie didn't know that. It felt and looked like a gun. They walked past the concierge's office and out into Primrose Hill Road. A car was there, but the man in it was someone Lizzie had never seen before, a big redhead in a leather coat and ragged jeans. The driver bundled her into the back.

Lizzie was so frightened she couldn't speak. She tried to, stammering and hesitating and gasping, but no real words came out. She wanted to ask her abductors where they were taking her, but it was useless to try. The redhead held her hands behind her back and put what felt like handcuffs on her wrists while the other man told her to bite on something he held across her mouth. She had seen this done on TV but had never thought how horrible it must feel, the bandage or scarf or whatever it was tied so tightly that it felt as if it must split her lips. The driver gave her a great shove so that she fell across the back seat with no hands free to struggle or defend herself.

The red-headed man took the gun from the driver, thrust it into her ribs and they were off. Few people were about, but even if the street had been crowded, Lizzie realised that people didn't look into parked cars, or moving cars for that matter. Not being able to use her hands made her into a disabled creature. It was the worst part of it. The gag was horrible, but only because it hurt, not because it made it impossible to utter a sound. She hadn't been able to speak before it went on and somehow she knew she wouldn't be able to speak now, even if they took it off. Would they remove the gag and the handcuffs when they got her to where they were taking her? If they didn't, the time might come when she wouldn't be able to go on breathing just through her nose. The thought of this made her give a little whimper, and the redhead hissed at her, 'Shut the fuck up.'

Like most Londoners, the only part of London Lizzie really knew was the bit round where she lived, in her case the area between Willesden and the Marylebone Road. They seemed quickly to have left that behind. Swithin would be ringing her doorbell now. Would he raise the alarm? Unlikely. A kind of fog spread across Lizzie's brain, although she was fully conscious, and she began to cry, tears falling down her cheeks on to the stretchy cotton stuff of the gag.

CHAPTER SEVENTEEN

'I know what you're going to say,' said Carl. 'I know it by heart. So don't bother. I could recite it. You don't have to say it.'

They were in Carl's bedroom on a Sunday afternoon, and Nicola had brought them two mugs of tea. Hers was half drunk, his untouched. Down below the window Sybil Soames was chopping down stinging nettles with shears while Dermot sat in one of the deckchairs reading what Nicola thought might be the parish magazine.

'I wouldn't put it past him to ask me to buy a lawnmower.'

'You have only to say no.'

'Look, the rent was due weeks ago, but it didn't come, and it won't. It won't come at all, will it? It will never come. At least he pays his gas and electricity bills, but he soon won't, you'll see. He'll ask me a favour, and the favour will be that I take on those bills.'

'Aren't you going to drink your tea?'

'No, I'm fucking not going to drink my tea.' He rolled

over and put his arms round her. 'I'm sorry. I shouldn't talk to you like that.'

It was a beautiful day. They walked across to Regent's Park, where it seemed the whole of London – except for those in Hyde, St James's and Green Park among others – was gathered, lying on the grass, playing ball games, eating and drinking, admiring the rose garden. The sun was hot, the leaves were green. Nature proclaimed that the winter had been mild and wet and the spring and summer warmer than usual.

'Suppose he starts rearranging my private life?' said Carl. 'What if he tells me that if you continue to live with me, he'll have to tell the Weatherspoon woman what I did? If he asks for the other bedroom, the one next to mine? What do I do then? I can't say no, can I?'

Nicola sighed. 'Carl, you know what I'll say to that.'

Even for a local weekly paper, the *Paddington Express* had a small circulation. But the current issue was selling better than any had for years. It led with the photograph of Stacey Warren that had previously appeared in the *Evening Standard* and various other dailies. The text surrounding it told of the dinitrophenol that had been obtained by Stacey not online but by buying it from 'an unknown source'.

Dermot was given a copy of the newspaper by Sybil, who knew nothing of the DNP story but wanted Dermot to see an ad for a second-hand bed to replace the broken-down one that had been Carl's father's. Carl's tenant, if such he still was, carefully left the newspaper on the table that was the only piece of furniture in the hallway of Falcon Mews.

The account in the *Paddington Express* didn't really say anything new. But Carl, who found the newspaper where Dermot intended him to find it, lead story headline uppermost, read everything into it that wasn't in fact there. He felt as though he was about to faint, though he had never fainted in his life. There was nowhere to sit down. He staggered dizzily into the living room and subsided into an armchair. Nicola had gone to work, as had Dermot.

Reason was disappearing. Carl was past the stage of looking calmly at the situation; long past. The sanity he clung to was that he knew he was being irrational. He knew that what Nicola said was true and that a rational person would do what she kept telling him to do. But with his increasing disgust at Dermot had come fear, and fear was now changing into terror. He was beginning to imagine horrible actions Dermot might take against him. This newspaper account was the beginning of them, for he had no doubt Dermot had fed the story to the *Paddington Express*. Probably even now he was passing the insinuations on to the *Evening Standard* or tomorrow's *Mail*. No imagining was needed for the takeover of his garden, the dropping and noisy shifting of pieces of furniture, the banging of doors and the spurts of music that gushed out for five minutes at a time when the front door to the top-floor flat was opened.

Carl found that going out and walking, especially in

green places and under the heavy-hanging foliage of trees, was somehow remedial. He could tell himself that whatever happened at home, however much Dermot tightened the screw and in so doing deprived him of every penny of his income, he would still have his health and strength and these green trees to walk under and lawns to look at. His walk this morning took him across Maida Vale and a little way down Lisson Grove in the direction of Rossmore Road. If he continued along Rossmore Road he would come out on to Park Road and from there on to the Outer Circle of Regent's Park. Plenty of greenery in there, great trees densely in leaf and shrubs in pink and white flower.

As he walked along Rossmore Road, a sign pointing to Jerome Crescent reminded him of something. Of course – Dermot's girlfriend Sybil Soames lived there with her parents. He turned into Jerome Crescent, where trees grew on a triangle of green grass, and decided to sit down there and wait for Sybil. She would come; she would be bound to come this way on her way home for her lunch. Somehow he knew she was the kind of girl – an only child sheltered and protected by her working-class parents – who would go shopping arm in arm with her mother on Saturday mornings, and on weekdays always go home for her lunch, which she would call dinner. Dermot, with his quaint outdated morality, would have had no difficulty in persuading her to go along with his wish for a chaste relationship. Carl asked himself why he wanted to talk to her – why he wanted to see her even – but came up with no answer.

She did come, but took a long time about it. He saw recognition and something that might have been fear in her eyes. She would have avoided him, turned off the path across the green, but for his saying, 'Sybil.'

On his feet now, he stood in front of her. 'Sybil, I've been waiting for you.'

'Is something wrong? Is he ill?'

You know what he's doing to me, don't you? Carl wanted to say. You know he's stopped paying me rent, he's taking over the house, he'll force me into one room and then out altogether. But confronted by Sybil, poor ignorant creature that she was, he couldn't do it. 'It's nothing,' he said. 'I just went for a walk and then I remembered you lived down here.' In a low, weak voice, quite wrong for such a cheerful remark, 'It's a beautiful day.'

'I'd better get on home,' she said. 'My mum'll be worrying.'

He watched her cross the road and turn into a doorway. Slowly making his way back up Lisson Grove, leaving behind all these pastel-painted blocks of flats and their green gardens, he realised again what he dreaded most in Dermot's threats. It wasn't the loss of income. It was the humiliation he feared. He couldn't live with the shame.

CHAPTER EIGHTEEN

At least she could see. They had deprived her of speech and to a great extent of movement, but neither of the men who had abducted Lizzie had blindfolded her, so she was able to lift her head high enough to see some street signs.

When – if – someone came to rescue her, they would want those sorts of clues to where she was. The car had gone over one of the river bridges and, for a moment, had drawn alongside a number 36 bus going north in the opposite direction. Lizzie thought fleetingly of her dad: could he be on the bus on his way back to Mamhead Drive? What would happen if he chanced to look over at the car and saw her – his only daughter – on the back seat, bound and gagged? But the traffic lights changed, and the bus moved on, and there was no help for her, no possibility of rescue. As her eyes filled once more with tears, she struggled to read the names of the places she was passing before, finally, the driver turned into an alley.

It occurred to Lizzie that these two men weren't very good criminals. They had the right sort of language and did the right sort of things, like putting on the gag and the handcuffs. But professional kidnappers, real criminals, wouldn't have left her eyes uncovered, they wouldn't have left her able to see everywhere they were taking her. Like the lane off Abbotswood Road where they were now, and the alley with its row of lock-up garages.

The driver must have used a remote, for the door of number 5 went up. Inside, the garage was empty and she could see there was no other way in or out of it. Lizzie thought they might speak to her now, but they didn't. They got out of the car, the driver first, then the redhead. It was then that she remembered a film she had seen of someone dying from being left in a car in a garage with carbon monoxide exuding from somewhere and poisoning them. Crying out or just crying was no use. She watched them moving out of the garage, leaving her inside the car, noting the height and size of them, their hair. And she thought of Swithin.

The garage door went down and closed, and deep darkness descended. When thinking about what to expect, Lizzie had forgotten darkness. She had forgotten air, too. But they must not want her to die, because the driver had left his door open a little way and the engine was turned off.

They would be back. They must be back.

Upstairs on the number 36 bus, heading north, Tom was thinking about his daughter. He'd long hoped for a change in her lifestyle and character, and now he clung to small steps towards improvement. She needed to find a nice young man with a job. Not a good job, not yet, that would be too much to ask in this day and age, but a man with a job in an office nine till five, and preferably Lizzie at home cooking his dinner. These flights of fancy continued until the bus reached Queen's Park and Tom got off to wait for one to take him to Willesden.

When the bus had dropped him at the end of Mamhead Drive and he was in the house, he learned from Dot that Lizzie was expected to supper. Also coming, though not exactly invited, was Eddy Burton from next door. His parents had moved in a month ago, and his mother was going out for the evening and had asked Dorothy if she would be kind enough to give him dinner. Tom thought feeding a man of twenty-eight who wasn't disabled or with learning difficulties was taking spoiling to an absurd extent. Surely Dot couldn't be matchmaking? Tom felt rather cross. He wanted to see his daughter on her own.

He didn't know how many times he had said to Lizzie that punctuality was the politeness of princes, yet still it was never any good expecting her at a specific time. He wondered if Prince Charles was punctual. He must be, with dozens of people fussing around to make sure he was on time for all those engagements. The Milsoms regularly ate at seven, and Lizzie was a Milsom, who knew their ways if anyone did.

Eddy had arrived early, bringing his pug with him, an uninvited guest, and had already got through a liberal helping of wine, pushing the empty glass into a prominent position where his hostess couldn't fail to see it. The pug, whose name was Brutus, ran around the room, leaping on to laps and licking faces. Dot refilled Eddy's glass, and Tom's. Clicking her tongue, not at all pleased, she phoned Lizzie's mobile.

The only answer she got was that the call had been transferred to a number consisting of about fifteen digits.

'She's forgotten,' said Tom. 'Or she's out with some bloke.'

Eddy looked embarrassed. He had been giving his hosts his dog's complicated life history, too complicated considering the animal was only eight months old, and both Tom and Dot were trying not to show their boredom.

'I suppose we'd better eat,' said Dorothy, and persuaded Eddy to shut the dog in the kitchen.

The doorbell rang in the middle of the lemon meringue pie course. Tom was sure it must be Lizzie and went to answer it with 'Lost your key, have you?' on his lips.

The roving fishmonger was on the doorstep, asking if Tom wanted some beautiful cod fresh out of the Atlantic that morning.

Dorothy phoned Lizzie again later, but again the voice-mail was transferred to that long number. Both she and Tom thought this meant that Lizzie had either gone home with the man she was no doubt out with, or had turned off her phone. They disliked the idea of her spending the night with a man, but they never said so, not even to each other. It was what girls did these days, and there was nothing to be done about it.

*

South of the river, Redhead and the squat little man who had been the driver came into the garage, switched a light on and opened the nearside rear door of the car. Lizzie heard Redhead call the other man Scotty, and thought how stupid he must be to reveal his name to her. Then, with a sob, she understood that he might do this if he didn't care if she knew his name. He didn't care because he meant to kill her.

Redhead got in the driving seat while Scotty got in the back with her. When he undid the gag, Lizzie had a strange feeling in her mouth and throat. It was like a block on her voice so that all she could do, no matter how she tried, was grunt and gasp like an animal.

'Gone loco,' said Scotty.

'Good. Don't want her screaming the fucking place down.'

The clock on the dashboard had showed Lizzie that it was a quarter past three in the morning. Redhead reversed the car out of the garage and into Abbotswood Road. In silence, Lizzie laid her head back against the upholstery.

Fear of urinating was keeping her silent and tense. She contracted her muscles as if they were fists closing tightly. It was called a sphincter, she thought; this was what kept her bladder holding it in. If her urine leaked out of her in front of them, she thought she would die. Tears trickled from her eyes. If only the water from her eyes would take some of the water that wanted to pour out of her bladder. Was that the way it worked? Redhead was turning the car into a row of marked-out parking places at the foot of a squalid-looking block of social housing. She had no idea where they were. She didn't care, concentrating only on holding her sphincter tight shut.

No one was about. Redhead and Scotty took her inside and up a flight of stone stairs, holding her between them. If someone had followed them, he or she would have seen the handcuffs still on Lizzie's wrists. No one was there to see.

Let into a flat by Scotty, she said, 'Toilet,' and Redhead pushed her through a door, slamming it behind her. The relief was so great, the *joy*, that for a moment she was almost happy, taking great breaths, indifferent to her cuffed hands, leaning her upper body forward to press on to her knees.

Scotty was outside the door, but even so she couldn't have gone anywhere. If your hands were tied behind your back, it was as bad as tying your feet, worse maybe. Scotty walked her into a living room, holding her shoulders. Redhead was in there, talking on his phone. He put it down when he saw her. Had he been talking to her parents?

'They haven't got any money,' Lizzie said.

'What you on about?' Scotty pushed her down on to a battered and ragged couch. 'He was talking to his husband.'

So they were gay. Or Redhead was. And very likely Scotty too. This comforted her. All the time she'd been in that car in the garage, she'd feared that one or both of them would rape her. Gay men wouldn't. 'What are you going to do with me?' she asked.

'You know something?' said Redhead. 'We're like the filth, we ask the questions, not you. You shut the fuck up.'

138

He produced a mobile phone and dropped it in her lap. He seemed to have forgotten she couldn't use it without her hands. Leaning towards her, his face very close to hers and his breath smelling of curry, he said, 'Tell me your mum's number.'

'I don't know what it is.'

Of course he didn't believe her. They gave her two pills after that, capsules really, half red and half green. Redhead held her down on the couch while Scotty forced the red and green things into her mouth, sitting on her legs and holding her lips crammed together with both hands. She swallowed them in saliva, not daring to hold them in her mouth.

Lizzie thought she would have a few minutes to take in the room in all its squalid detail, note that outside it was now getting light, but unconsciousness was coming fast. She just had time to wonder why Redhead had asked for her mum's phone number, and not her mum and dad's, when a black door slammed over her eyes and she passed out.

CHAPTER NINETEEN

Tom and Dot were vaguely concerned that they had still not heard from Lizzie, but they had become used to her disappearing for days on end, only to find that she hadn't really disappeared, just gone off to lead her own life. And she was of course a young woman in her twenties, not a teenager any longer.

Tom had observed, with interest, that when your child is living in the parental home, you worry when she is out in the evening after eleven, say. You are worried sick if she is still out after midnight. You watch the clock and pace and open the front door every ten minutes to try and spot her coming down the street. Sleep is out of the question. But when she is no longer living at home, although you know she goes out in the evenings just as much, stays out just as late, if not later, you scarcely worry at all. You go to bed and sleep. You wake up in the morning and have no doubt – if you even think about it – that she came in at midnight or one or two, safe and sound. Why was this? Why did you worry when she was living with you but not when she wasn't?

He had asked other parents about this, and they all felt the same.

'She probably got the wrong day and thinks she's due here to supper on Friday rather than last night,' he said to Dot. 'She'll turn up.'

Lizzie awoke to broad daylight. It hadn't been a natural awakening. One of them – Scotty, she thought – had shaken her while the other pressed an ice-cold rag against her face. It felt as if it had been in the freezer.

'We want a phone number,' Redhead said.

'But I haven't got my bag. I haven't got my phone. How can I have a number?'

'You've got a memory, haven't you? You know your own mum's number.'

What had her mother to do with anything, Lizzie thought, and why would she give these obviously violent men her parents' number? 'I don't know,' she lied. 'I don't know. I can't remember.'

Her voice was breaking again. She tried to say she couldn't think, but the words wouldn't come. Scotty slapped her face hard and she burst into howls. Her hands were shaking in the cuffs, which were wet with sweat. Yvonne, she thought suddenly. She took deep breaths in and out as slowly as she could as she thought about Stacey's beautiful flat, and how unfair it was that Yvonne, who had her own mansion in Swiss Cottage, had inherited this too.

No, she decided in a fit of spite, she wouldn't give Scotty

and Redhead her mum's number; she'd give them Yvonne's instead. She knew her telephone number too, and could almost visualise it from when she'd seen it on the pet-clinic computer screen that day. Closing her eyes and concentrating hard, she recited the number to her captors.

A little path runs down from Lisson Grove, a short cut into the pink- and green- and blue-painted blocks that fill the area north of Rossmore Road. Nicola and Carl had walked through the Church Street market, bought some fruit and a couple of avocados, which Carl put in his backpack.

Nicola was surprised to see the antique shops at the other end of Church Street. She had never been there before and wanted to go into every shop. They held no interest for Carl, but once inside, the various vases and urns and small pieces of furniture caught his attention, even distracting him momentarily from his general despair. A chess set of which half the big chessmen were carved from golden wood and the other half from white attracted him so much that if he'd had the money he would have liked to buy it. The cost would have been beyond his means at any time.

Nicola fell in love, as she put it, with a green goose in a shop called Tony's Treasury. It was an ornament of no possible use, but it had its charm, being made of pottery, green with white edges to each of its feathers and a purple head with red wattles and beak. It was big, rotund, the size of a football and very heavy to lift.

'It would look lovely on your hall table,' she said. 'I'll buy it for you.'

Impossible to say he didn't want it and equally impossible to get up much enthusiasm. He didn't ask how much it was but found out when he saw her hand the shop-owner two twenty-pound notes and a ten. The goose was so heavy he had to carry it in his backpack with the groceries.

They crossed Lisson Grove and he led the way down the little path that ultimately brought them into Jerome Crescent. These streets here, Carl thought, could aptly be called respectable. They were clean, the buildings in a good state of decoration and the postcode one of the most prestigious in London. No one called the blocks council flats any more – it would have been politically incorrect – but that was what they were.

'Up there is where Sybil Soames lives.' It was the first thing Carl had said to her since they left the antique shop. 'That bastard's girlfriend. Those flats that are painted green, that's where she lives with her mum and dad.'

Nicola followed his gaze. She took in the bicycle on the balcony and the net curtains. 'You only call them that because you're a snob. You'd call them her mother and father if you didn't despise them.'

He said nothing. He was looking at the yellow nasturtiums in a flower bed, the scaffolding on the block opposite the green one and the stack of bricks on the pathway. The goose in the backpack weighed heavily on his shoulders.

'Why did we come here?' she asked.

'Something seems to draw me to this place,' he said. 'I can't get away from him, you see. And he's here. He may be up there now. I dream about him. I don't want to let him out of my sight and yet I hate him. I loathe him.'

'Oh, Carl.' She took his arm, held it and clutched his hand. 'What shall we do?'

'What you want me to do I can't do. I never will. Come on. Let's go home.'

As they walked back to Falcon Mews, along the sunlit streets, under the green trees, Carl became increasingly agitated, uttering angry denunciations of Dermot, cursing him, going over once again, twice, three times, what had happened and what his tenant had done.

Nicola kept silent; she had nothing to say because she had said it all. Now she was thinking what she must do. Should she force Carl to take some drastic step, perhaps? Leave the house in Falcon Mews, rent a room for both of them, find himself a regular day job? Or should she abandon him, leave him behind? She thought, I used to love him – do I still love him? He hardly speaks but to rage against Dermot. He sleeps a little, dreams violently, cries out and sits up fighting against something that isn't there. I would be better without him, but would he be better without me? She didn't know the answer.

How pretty Falcon Mews was on a sunny day. The little houses were all of different shapes and heights, their roofs of grey slate or red tile, their windows diamond-paned or plate glass in white frames, some walls covered in variegated ivy or long-leaved clematis. Flowers were everywhere, sprays and bunches of them hanging on the climbers amid festoons of dark green leaves. It was all so lovely, a beautiful place to live and be happy in. They went into the house, into the dim silence. Carl put the food and drink into the fridge, took the backpack upstairs and dropped it on the bedroom floor.

Nicola was looking out of the kitchen window into the back garden, where she could see Dermot in one of the deckchairs reading a magazine. Sybil had acquired a pair of lawn trimmers and was cutting the edges, where the grass met the flower beds where the nettles used to be. She was the kind of woman, Nicola thought, who always had to be doing something: weeding, cutting, chopping, cooking, cleaning – a gift to a man. Carl was silent now, but when he saw those two, as he must sooner or later, he would start his agonised complaints again. She couldn't leave him, but nor could she put up with him much longer.

Suppose she did what Dermot hadn't yet done and might never do? Only she and he knew the truth of what had happened on the day Carl sold the DNP to Stacey Warren. If she told the whole story to a newspaper, and if, say, the *Paddington Express* used it and passed it to the *Evening Standard*, it would be in the public domain – wasn't that what they called it? – just as much as if Dermot had told them. Dermot wouldn't have been responsible for its appearance, she would, but the effect would be the same. Dermot would no longer have anything to hold over Carl. His inverted blackmail would no longer work. He would therefore be obliged to pay Carl's rent once more or leave. Also, Carl might demand rent arrears and surely get them. Once that had been done, he could evict Dermot.

And what of her? She would have to tell Carl it was she who had – well, betrayed him. He might never want to see her again, but as things were, she couldn't continue with him like this. She went to the fridge and opened the still rather warm white wine they had bought in Church Street – well, not they; it was she who had bought it. Carl had almost run out of money.

She poured the wine and carried in the glasses and found Carl at the back window, looking through a barrier of leaves and branches and privet bushes at Sybil chopping away at the lawn edge and Dermot apparently sleeping in his deckchair.

Carl took the glass and gulped down half of its contents, the way he always drank these days. Nicola drank more slowly, studying the man she still loved, wondering what she should do.

CHAPTER TWENTY

Dermot wasn't in love with Sybil, but aspects of her pleased him very much. She reminded him of his mother, always busy, never sitting down for long except in church. A woman should have a faith, he thought now; women needed religion more than men. She spent a lot of time in his flat but he hardly ever saw her relax. Washing machines, microwaves and freezers held no attraction for her. 'Made for lazy people' was how she described them. When she had finished doing his washing by hand and putting up a line to peg it out on, she settled down with his mending. Even his mother no longer mended socks or sewed on buttons, though he remembered her doing his father's darning when he was a little boy. Sybil cooked his dinner on Saturdays and Sundays too, and it was the old-fashioned food he liked: roast beef and Yorkshire pudding and shepherd's pie. Until now he had never thought about getting married, but that might have been because he had never met a girl he could contemplate marrying.

One thing he particularly liked about Sybil was that

she had never shown any kind of sexual interest in him. He had started kissing her, because that was what you did with a girl, but only on the cheek. Holding hands was something else he did with her, and she seemed to like it. He didn't know, because he had never put it to the test, how having sexual relations would be with her or anyone else. But he was convinced he would only be able to perform this duty if they were married. Then it would be all right. But it would be far from all right and would fail if he attempted it before marriage, because that would be immoral.

He was thinking along these lines and resolving to ask Sybil to marry him when Yvonne Weatherspoon walked into the pet clinic with Sophie in her cat box.

'I haven't got an appointment, I know,' she said quickly. 'There's nothing really wrong with her, but I thought maybe Caroline would give her her injections, you know, for worms and fleas and whatever, even though it's a few weeks early.'

'Maybe Melissa can, I'll enquire.' Dermot did, and got an exasperated agreement. Yvonne was one of their more demanding clients. She needed more attention than Sophie.

Yvonne took Sophie out of the box and held her in her arms, closely snuggled.

'Better not,' said Dermot. 'We had a cat escape last week when a client opened the door – no more than an inch or two, but you know what cats are.'

Yes, she knew what cats were: highly intelligent, beautiful and good. Very reluctantly, Yvonne put Sophie back in the box. 'Nasty Dermot's a real spoilsport. We need our cuddles, don't we?'

Dermot was still thinking about what form the question he planned to ask Sybil should take. Of course he wouldn't be asking her yet; it was Tuesday, and they only met at the weekends and on Friday evenings. They had discovered quite early in their relationship that they were in perfect agreement on this subject. Both worked hard, went to bed early and got up early. Otherwise, how could they do their jobs properly? That was what weekends were for, relaxing (in his case) or catching up on all the domestic tasks that needed to be done (in hers). Yes, he thought, she would make him a good wife. A good old-fashioned wife, none of your post-impressionist feminist partners, or whatever they called them. Would he have to buy her a ring? That was something to give some thought to. They could live in the flat for the first few years, and then maybe he could buy a house in Winchmore Hill or Oakwood.

Nicola had found a website for the *Paddington Express*. It had offices in Eastbourne Terrace, walking distance from Falcon Mews. With all the contact information in hand, her plan of action seemed real. She would go there and ask to see the editor (or news editor or features editor), and she or he would be very interested, record what Nicola had to say and perhaps take it down in shorthand as well. Did people still use shorthand? They would ask if they could send a photographer round. They would find out that Carl didn't know she was telling them what he had done. It wasn't as simple as it had seemed at first. It now appeared almost treacherous. If she did this, she would have lost him. This must be the end.

Perhaps she wouldn't have to do it herself. Or not do it in person. She could send an anonymous letter. Nicola marvelled that she, who was surely an honest, decent sort of person, should even contemplate such a thing. Perhaps honest, decent people imagined this kind of behaviour, but they didn't carry it out. Of course they didn't. When the time came, she would go herself and be straightforward and truthful. There was nothing else for it. The only question was when.

Yvonne Weatherspoon arranged the white-chocolate-coated circular shortbread biscuits she knew she shouldn't eat, and therefore restricted herself to one a day, on an oval china plate. She put the plate on a tray with the coffee pot and two cups, the jug of semi-skimmed milk and the two sachets of sugar substitute. The thin milk and thinner little packets were to make up for the biscuits.

Yvonne was setting the tray on the table by the open French windows when the landline rang. She picked it up.

A coarse voice, quite a rough male voice, said, 'Mrs Weatherspoon? Mrs Yvonne Weatherspoon?'

'Yes?'

'We've got your daughter. She's OK at present, and you can have her back . . .' the man paused to speak to someone, 'for a lot of money.'

Yvonne laughed. 'That's very funny, as my daughter is sitting here beside me. You can speak to her if you like.'

The phone was abruptly cut off.

Yvonne and Elizabeth agreed on few things, but this was one of them. They both laughed, Elizabeth hysterically, Yvonne with more restraint. 'Do you think we should tell the police?'

'I don't think so,' Elizabeth said. 'Let sleeping cops lie.'

'Are you going to set me free now?' Lizzie asked, using a phrase she had learned from a TV drama about royalty in the thirteenth century.

Scotty and Redhead looked a bit rattled, she thought, as though their plan hadn't gone entirely as they had expected.

'Why would we do that? That wasn't your mum, just as you must have known it wouldn't be.' Redhead fetched her a mug of water. 'We're going to have to move you, so we're going to give you enough pills to knock you out for twenty-four hours.' A faint smile crossed his face. 'Don't say we don't look after you.'

'Would you put the cuffs on my hands in front?' she asked, feeling alarmed. 'Please.'

But the handcuffs remained where they were, and soon the two men appeared to be ready to leave, Redhead with a suitcase and a big holdall, and Scotty with a bottle that must contain the sleeping pills. He shook not two but three of them into his hand and signed to her to put her head back and open her mouth.

What's the maximum safe dose? Lizzie wondered, but she opened her mouth and swallowed the pills, washing them down with the rest of the water in the mug.

They walked her downstairs, both supporting her, talking as they went, grumbling about who they had thought she was, and what they were going to do with her now.

The car was in a side entrance outside a back door. Consciousness was going and Lizzie stumbled down the last few steps, wondering vaguely what time it was, early or late, as blackness and oblivion descended.

When she came round, to use her father's phrase, her hands were shackled in front and cable had been tightly tied round her feet.

While captive, she was learning things. When you feel comfortable in your body, most of the time you're barely aware of having a body. But when part of it is tied up, hands together and feet together, you feel stiff and then you start to ache. You wonder if this is what it will be like when you're old. Recovering consciousness, you don't feel wide awake quickly; for a long time you feel weak and feeble and vague and the room swims around you.

To keep her weight down, Lizzie had eaten sparingly for months, years really, so she had got used to small meals and hadn't often felt hungry. But she had in the past eaten something every day and had never felt like this. Her hunger was a devouring presence. Although she knew it was a stupid thing to do, she couldn't stop herself imagining her mother's cooking, so that she actually saw before her eyes her famous lemon meringue pie, the glistening leg of lamb surrounded by potatoes roasted in goose fat, the apple tart with its latticed lid. She had never till now known what it meant to have your mouth water. Now she did.

It amazed her that she could do without a bath or a shower. She was still wearing the same clothes she had worn when Scotty and Redhead took her away, and inside Stacey's black dress with the white lace panel, filthy now and torn, her body smelled like a sick dog and her hair as if it had been buried in dusty earth. But all this worried her less than she would ever have expected. If she smelt bad, so did Redhead and Scotty.

In this new place, she was left alone, drugged, given water when she woke but no food apart from a piece of white bread from a sliced loaf and a hunk of cheese in the morning and the evening. One of them took her to the bathroom when they brought the bread and slammed the door on her, waiting outside. She had to shuffle along slowly because of the rope tied around her ankles. They no longer spoke to her.

She had no idea of how much time had passed when they took her downstairs again, put her in the car, and drove her through dark, winding streets to a new prison.

The previous year, in late July, when school was finished and the little ones were supervised by volunteer mothers, Lizzie had gone off somewhere on

157

a holiday with a friend or friends. Or she said she had, but you never knew when she was telling the truth and when she was not.

These were Tom's thoughts, not Dot's. Tom no longer believed much of what Lizzie said, while Dot always had faith in her daughter. More than this, though, she trusted and believed in what her husband said. If Tom said Lizzie was somewhere on the Mediterranean, or in Cornwall, that was where she was. While it annoyed Tom that his daughter would disappear somewhere with friends and not tell him or her mother where she was, it upset Dorothy.

'She's an adult,' he said. 'She has her own life.'

'I knew you'd say that. Of course you're right, but I think she could ring us. It's not much to ask.'

'You've never asked her, though, have you? Maybe you should. I doubt it'll make any difference, but it would set your mind at rest – in the future. To know where she was.'

'Oh, it is at rest. I'm not worried, I'm cross.'

But she was worried, and so was he. They might have confided in each other, but they never did that. Each pretended that Lizzie must be safe somewhere and fine. Unpleasant things happened to young girls every day, the newspapers said so, but they did their best to dismiss this thought. Nothing nasty could ever happen to their Lizzie.

CHAPTER TWENTY-TWO

It had become an obsession. Carl understood that his behaviour was just as much that of a fanatical lover as of a fixated hater. He followed Dermot with his eyes whenever he had the opportunity, listened for what he could hear of him, outside the door at the top of the stairs: his music, his footsteps, and his words on the phone or when he spoke to Sybil Soames. When Dermot approached the door, Carl ran down the top flight of stairs to hide in his own bedroom.

At first he did this only while Nicola was at work, but gradually he came hardly to care at all. Anyway, she knew. She had told him what he should do, but now she had stopped; telling him, she said, was useless. Probably the time was coming when she would give up on him and leave. He wouldn't care. Sometimes he thought he wouldn't even notice.

Once or twice he had followed Dermot to work. If Dermot had turned round and seen him, he wouldn't have cared, but he didn't turn round. Carl watched as

Dermot went into the pet clinic by a back door. Then the clinic lights came on and he walked away.

He had also begun to follow Dermot to Sybil's parents' house when he walked her home in the evenings. Occasionally, if it was raining or chilly, Dermot called a taxi for her. He could easily afford taxis now, Carl thought bitterly. But mostly he set off with Sybil at about nine thirty in the evening. They held hands. Or rather, Dermot held her hand. She wouldn't have dared take his, Carl thought.

Their walk took about twenty minutes and they always went the same way: down Castellain Road, into Clifton Gardens and across Maida Vale into St John's Wood Road to Lisson Grove. They kept always to those same wide roads and never took the short cut along the canal path. Although it was lit, it was much darker along there, a lovers' walk under the trees. Did Dermot avoid it with Sybil for that reason? Because it was somehow intimate, sheltered, a place for kissing?

On the way back though, he did go that way. After he had kissed Sybil's cheek, watched her go into the flats, waved once, he turned round and took the little path that went over the canal bridge and led along the dark water. He walked very slowly, pausing to look down on to the glassy canal.

Carl watched from the other side of Lisson Grove. When he was at university, he had belonged to the dramatic society, and the high spot of his second year had been their performance of *Measure for Measure*. A line came back to him, a phrase really, 'the duke of dark corners'. Dermot looked like that, with his round shoulders and long, thin neck; almost a medieval figure, dressed in a dark jacket, black jeans tucked into black boots. Under the bridge at Lisson Grove and under the bridge at Aberdeen Place were dark corners, footpaths melting into blackness.

If Carl wondered about Dermot, why he always walked to Jerome Crescent the way he did and returned along the towpath, he also wondered at himself. What made him follow Dermot? What did he get out of it? He didn't know. He just had a compulsion to do it.

Nicola had gone back to her old flat and the girls for the night, and he was sitting in his bedroom in the dark when he heard Dermot come in. These days he seldom thought about anything but Dermot, and sometimes Sybil, but pushing his backpack into a corner with his foot, he noticed that Nicola hadn't taken the goose out to put it on the hall table.

Sunday, and Dermot had come back from church with Sybil and a crowd of other people. Carl, watching from upstairs, saw him unlock the front door and welcome them all in. It was another fine day, clouds across the blue sky but plenty of sunshine too. There were two women among them, apart from Sybil, and all wore bright floral dresses. Sybil's had a pattern on it of pink cabbage roses on a black background. The door shut with a bang.

Nicola was out, at a brunch with two of her ex-flatmates.

He had forgotten to mention the goose. Never mind. It wasn't important. Nothing was but Dermot and maybe money.

He went into his bedroom and looked out of the window, hoping that Dermot and his guests wouldn't go into the garden. No one was out there, but as he turned away, he heard a commotion from downstairs as they all burst out among the flowers. Gusts of laughter drifted up. Sybil appeared with the trolley that had been Carl's father's, loaded with bottles and cans and plates of food and packets of crisps. Everyone started eating and drinking. Sybil was walking among them holding up her left hand for them to see something. Someone said, 'I know you'll be very happy.' Not 'I hope', but 'I know'.

It was an engagement party. Carl felt sick. He fell back into a chair. 'Don't let him see you,' he said aloud, and then whispered it. 'Don't let him see you, he'll ask you down. He'll tell you his news and ask you to join them.'

Very quietly, as if they were all listening for him to make a move, he crept into the bathroom and drank from the cold tap above the sink.

Nicola had said nothing about coming back that evening, but he expected her. Even if those people were still in the garden, still eating and drinking, her return would be a comfort. He would ask her about the goose – did she really want it? He didn't care if there was an ornament on the hall table or not.

He had eaten no lunch, had eaten nothing, and there

was no wine in the house. In the kitchen was half a loaf of bread and a piece of cheese left over from last evening's dinner. He lay on the bed and fell asleep, overcome with despair. At some point in the afternoon or early evening – it was still light – he was awakened by the party guests going home. They weren't especially noisy, he had to admit that, but the slightest sound would have disturbed him. He got up and watched them go.

The sky had clouded over and a wind got up. The tree branches in Falcon Mews swayed and all the leaves fluttered. A blackbird was singing somewhere and a magpie making its repetitive squawk. He searched for his phone but it had run out of charge. If Nicola didn't come, bringing food, he would have to go out and buy himself something to eat. Though it was Sunday, all the shops round here stayed open till late.

He picked up the backpack and its weight told him the goose was still inside. He'd take it back to Tony's Treasury, he decided, and see what he would give him for it.

He heard Dermot's footsteps on the stairs, and Sybil's. He wouldn't be walking her home yet but maybe taking her out to dinner. Some snack at one of the cafés on the Edgware Road, Carl thought contemptuously. This would be an evening when he wouldn't follow them. Nicola had left some money in a jacket pocket: a twenty-pound note and five pound coins. He wrote on an orange Post-it he took from a pad in the other pocket, *Borrowed £25. XX.* That would be enough to get something to eat in case Tony refused to buy back the green goose.

Dermot and Sybil had disappeared when he came out into the mews. No one was about except for Mr Kaleejah and his dog. He took that dog out three or four times a day. It was carrying a rubber bone in its mouth. Carl walked along Sutherland Avenue and across Maida Vale into Hall Road, and from there into Lisson Grove, where a crowd was coming out of the Roman Catholic church. There was a Tesco in Church Street that would still be open. But Tony's Treasury wasn't. Carl hadn't anticipated this. That Tony might refuse to take the goose back, yes, that was possible, but not for his shop to be closed. The Tesco was open, though, and still had a couple of Sunday papers on the rack outside. He bought a loaf of bread, a piece of Cheddar, a bar of chocolate and a half-bottle of rosé, using the money he'd taken from Nicola.

Carl wanted to avoid seeing Dermot. He didn't think Dermot would be near the canal, but when he and Sybil had eaten they would walk back to Jerome Crescent via the little path that ran from Lisson Grove. So Carl followed a route that was new to him, into Lisson Green where the canal came out from under the Aberdeen Place bridge. The water was dark here, the path along the bank deserted. He also noticed that you could see the path from Lisson Grove, and see too where the canal disappeared under the next bridge on its way through Regent's Park.

He sat down on a wooden bench and ate some bread and cheese. He was surprised to find how hungry he was. The path continued to be deserted. After a while, he made his way into Paveley Street. It was there, looking for a path out, that he saw Dermot and Sybil up ahead in Jerome Crescent, entering the block where Sybil lived. Going to continue the engagement celebrations, Carl thought bitterly.

Lights were on in a couple of windows in Sybil's block. Carl sat down on the stack of bricks. He didn't know why. He certainly wasn't waiting for Dermot. He didn't understand what it was that brought him here so regularly to watch what Dermot did, what they both did, as if they were fascinating people whose activities were of enormous interest, rather than the reverse.

He got up and walked round the block, round Jerome Crescent and back. As he watched, a light in one of the windows went out, then the other one. He moved into deep shadow as Dermot appeared at the entrance, then emerged into the half-light and crossed the street towards him.

'Hello there. What brings you here?' Dermot sounded surprised.

'I've got something to show you,' Carl said. 'I've brought you a present.'

'That's awfully decent of you,' said Dermot, like a public school boy of a hundred years ago. 'For my engagement, is it?'

'That's right.' Carl suddenly decided to give him the goose. He didn't know why he'd said he had a present. Just an odd impulse. He bent over the backpack and started unzipping it. For a brief moment while Dermot watched, anticipating his present, Carl began taking the goose out, then abruptly he lifted the backpack as high as he could, and brought it down hard on Dermot's head. He was taller than Dermot, and there was a crunch of bone.

Dermot uttered a long, dull groan. It was the only sound he made as he slumped over on to the pavement.

Careful not to touch Dermot, Carl bent over him to see whether he was still breathing. He didn't appear to be. Then Carl picked up the bag. He couldn't see any blood. Perhaps it was too dark, or there wasn't any. He hoisted the backpack on to his shoulders and for some reason looked at the windows that had been lit up. Both were still in darkness, though he fancied he saw a faint flicker of movement behind the higher one. He thought, why did I never think of doing this before? For months I've been desperate to get rid of this awful threat, this burden. He felt no guilt, no regret. He felt relief.

He walked away and up the path into Lisson Grove. It was as well the backpack was on his back, because his hands were shaking so much as to be useless for carrying anything. He climbed up the hill past the Catholic church, turned into Lodge Road and walked along beside the high walls above the railway line. Walking was automatic, his legs carrying him mechanically towards a safer place. A single cyclist rode past him and up to cross Park Road. Carl went across the road after him and down a path into the green, the trees, the dense leafiness that clustered and shivered in the rising wind along the canal bank. The water was black and still and shiny.

He hoisted the backpack off his shoulders, unzipped

it and lifted out the green goose. Something dark was on his hands, but whether it was blood or not, he couldn't tell. He looked about him into the trees above, the leaves making a soft whispering sound. The screen of branches that hid the road running alongside Regent's Park was dense and dark. The man on the bike had disappeared, was no doubt far away now, heading for Primrose Hill or Camden Town. Carl knelt down on the canal bank and dropped the backpack into the water. It floated for a few moments, then sank with a sucking, glugging sound.

He remained on his knees for perhaps two minutes holding the goose, then got to his feet with difficulty, like an old man, feeling about him in vain for something to hold on to. Carrying the goose under one arm, he started to walk back. He climbed up into Park Road and thought, without quite knowing why, that it would be better to go back along the St John's Wood Road rather than Lodge Road.

It started to rain, a drizzle at first, blown about by the wind, but soon it changed to a great storm. Good, Carl thought, it would wash Dermot's blood off him, although he was pretty sure what little there was had been on the backpack. He could feel the rain lashing against him, and streaming down his back and legs. It changed him from being mildly warm to a sudden sharp cold, and a huge weariness took hold of him, an exhaustion so powerful that he stumbled as he walked.

The rain had driven home those people who had been in the streets. Sutherland Avenue was deserted, apart from the Tesco supermarket, where cars still came and went, skidding through puddles. Turning into Castellain Road and staggering to the corner of the mews, he found himself dreading that Dermot might be there, waiting inside the front door to make some fatuous remark. Then he remembered.

No Dermot. Never again. But Nicola was there, opening the door just as he reached out with his key. She took one look at his sodden clothes and without asking him why he was carrying her green goose, put her arms round him and pulled him inside.

CHAPTER TWENTY-THREE

They were going to move Lizzie again. For some reason they were in a hurry and packing stuff into bags and boxes, and they'd forgotten to give her the pills. It wasn't much help – her hands were still shackled and her ankles tied – but at least her head was clear. She thought, they'll remember in a minute and then they'll drug me, but it seemed they thought she'd had the pills, for they dragged her down the stairs, clutching her arms painfully and roughly, and bundled her into the back seat of their car. It was broad daylight, but nobody was nearby. Had anybody seen her, they would have thought she was just another drunken woman and would have taken very little notice.

She didn't know where they were taking her, only that it was like countryside here, with broad areas of grass and big trees. She didn't recognise it, but they must have thought she did, because Redhead pulled in to the side of the road and stopped, and Scotty got into the back and tied a scarf round her eyes. The smell of him so close was bad, but she must smell as foul, for while she could still see, she saw him flinch away from her.

Now that her head was clear, Lizzie considered her position, and not for the first time. Could Swithin Campbell be behind her abduction? she wondered. Was that even his real name? She'd invited him into Stacey's flat, had wanted him to think she was well off. Could he and Redhead and Scotty have mistaken her for Yvonne's daughter, another Elizabeth? And now that they all knew she wasn't the Elizabeth they'd supposed her to be, what was going to happen to her?

They drove on, through open spaces or streets, she could no longer tell. They were all out of the car and halfway up a path when she thought she had a chance of escape, but her ankles were still tied and the single hobbled step she took resulted in her sprawling. Redhead picked her up with rough hands, and once they were inside a door, slapped her face on both cheeks painfully. The scarf was pulled off and she was dragged upstairs to a single room at the top.

Most people of Lizzie's age would not have been able to identify the type of dwelling she was in. They would have known it was old and small and that was about it. She hardly knew why she bothered to amass all this stuff in her head. Why did she care? Perhaps she thought it might be useful to know once she got out of here. If she got out.

She got off the bed where they had dumped her and, wide awake for the first time since she had become their prisoner, stumbled across to the window.

She was in the kind of cottage her grandmother had lived in. Such small terraced or sometimes semi-detached houses are to be found in every London suburb, tucked away among blocks of flats, tall Victorian terraces and large single houses. A few are still occupied by a solitary elderly resident; others have been bought by young couples who have smartened them up and filled them with the latest equipment.

This cottage, Lizzie saw, had been lived in by someone of her grandmother's generation. She could tell by the single bed and the cover on it called an eiderdown, the two little armchairs with cushions on their seats shaped like doughnuts, and the twenty or thirty tiny ornaments on the mantelpiece: china dogs, a brass bell, two framed photographs and a number of unidentifiable objects. She thought this old lady – for it was surely a woman – must have died and left the house to a relation, perhaps Redhead or Scotty's mother, and that was how they happened to have possession of it.

The window was large, far too large for the cottage, and although it had been put in perhaps only ten years previously, the frame looked jerry-built and rotten. The curtains, pink roses on a blue and green background, were drawn, and Lizzie pulled them back so that she looked out on to what seemed to be a public park. She could, she realised, be anywhere south of the river Thames, a vast area of London she barely knew. Below her were tall trees, smaller trees and bushes, tennis courts, paths winding among flower beds, people strolling. Birds in the trees, English ones, and those green parakeets that were

English now, having come here to live and settled down happily.

She thought, feeling happier suddenly, tomorrow they will let me go. I know it, but I don't know how I do. She sat down in one of the little armchairs and swung her bound legs up on to the other chair. It is almost as easy to untie a knot in a rope with cuffed hands as with free ones, and she had this one undone in seconds. Someone would be bound to come in, so she sat where she was with the rope tied loosely round her ankles and waited. Someone did come. It was Redhead, with a plate of chips and a can of Diet Coke. He didn't speak as he took off her cuffs, allowing her to eat, and he didn't even glance at her ankles.

As he was leaving she said, 'Where's the bathroom?'

'Downstairs. I'm not taking you.'

Once she would have argued, pleaded, even cried. Not now. She thought of the old woman who had lived here, waited till Redhead had gone, and looked under the bed. It was there, a china chamber pot, as she had once heard someone call it. She would have to use it, and worse, leave it for one of them to empty. The alternative was to pour the contents out of the window. People used to do that, she had read in a social history book, in the days when there was no plumbing.

Revelling in the fact that her hands were free for the first time in days, she used the pot and pushed it back under the bed, so as not to have to see it. Then she lay down under the eiderdown and thought about the old and the poor who not so long ago had used chamber

172

pots and carried big pottery jugs of hot water to fill bowls for washing in. It was the first time she had thought about something other than herself and her plight. For some unaccountable reason, going to bed with an almost empty stomach on top of a pot full of urine in a stuffy room no longer seemed a dreadful fate. It would pass, she knew; it would soon end.

It must have been four or five in the morning when the crash woke her. Outside it was getting light, and a large pane from the window in her room had been smashed. Most of it was lying in shards on her bed.

Lizzie got up and put on her shoes before making her way to the window, glass crunching under her feet. Standing there looking down, she heard thuds and bangs as Scotty and Redhead ran downstairs. Seconds later they both appeared carrying bags and hoisting backpacks and ran up the street in search of their car. They were abandoning her.

What had caused the crash? Had someone fired a gun at the window? Had something exploded? Scotty and Redhead evidently thought so. Lizzie knew she must leave as quickly as she could in spite of the early hour, in spite of Stacey's soiled black and white dress. She opened the door of the wardrobe – on the off chance, her grandmother would have said. Nothing was inside but a padded jacket, shiny, purple but not dirty. It could have belonged to anyone, but no matter. She put it on.

It was only at this point that she remembered she had no money, no bus or tube pass, no credit card. But she didn't care. Freedom was the main thing, and she had freedom. She went downstairs. The front door was open, and out in the street there was no one but a young man pulling a case on wheels along a path in the park. It didn't matter which way she walked, though it made sense to go in the opposite direction from Scotty and Redhead.

She saw what must have caused her smashed window. The biggest pigeon she had ever seen had flown straight into the glass and lay dead, a shining mass of blue and green and gold and brown feathers, on the pavement.

'Oh, poor bird,' said Lizzie aloud, tears in her eyes. She bent down and picked up the dead pigeon and laid it on the grass just inside the park gate, covering it as best she could with leaves.

She walked along painfully in Stacey's ridiculous high heels, and read on a street name the postcode SE13. Where that was, beyond its being south-east London, she had no idea. There might be a tube station, though, and there would certainly be buses, but neither would be of any use to her with no pass and no cards and no money.

What she could do came to her quite suddenly, and she thought what a fool she had been not to have thought of it before. The sole form of transport you paid for only at the end of the journey was a taxi.

CHAPTER TWENTY-FOUR

Tom and Dot were still trying not to feel anxious about Lizzie.

It was Dot's belief that she must be somewhere on holiday. Cornwall was a likely choice, because Lizzie knew someone whose parents lived there. Tom fixed on Barcelona. It was very popular with young people; indeed, he'd read that visitor numbers – formerly about a million a year – had increased sevenfold in recent years. But another day had come and brought no Lizzie with it.

They got up an hour or so later than usual on weekend mornings, having always done so when Tom worked, so Dot happened to be standing at their bedroom window at twenty past eight on Sunday morning, drawing back the curtains, when a black cab pulled up outside their gate. A girl she didn't at first recognise got out of it and ran up the path. She was young, with straggly caramel-blonde hair, and a short black and white dress covered by a cheap shiny padded jacket probably bought from a market stall. Even from this distance she looked dirty, very dirty.

It was Lizzie.

Tom was sitting up in bed, drinking the tea Dot had brought him. 'Our daughter is at the front door,' Dot told him. And then, using a phrase popular with her own mother, 'She looks as if she's been pulled through a hedge backwards.'

The door was opened to admit a Lizzie even dirtier than she had looked from upstairs. 'Mum, can you pay the man?' she said. 'It's a terrible lot but I haven't any money.'

'How much?'

'Thirty-five pounds.'

'I don't believe it,' said Dot, who did.

In the house, Lizzie said she'd pay her back but was first going to have a bath and wash her hair. Dot didn't ask her where she had been or why she was dirty and without money. As for Lizzie, she wasn't sure what she would tell her parents about what had happened to her.

Lying in the bath, she came to a decision. If she told her parents the truth, they would only make a fuss. Without a doubt, they would want to inform the police. She would be asked awkward questions that she might struggle to answer, like why was she living in Stacey's flat, drinking her drink, wearing her clothes? She couldn't also help feeling a little complicit in her own abduction: had she not wanted people to believe she was someone else; someone a lot wealthier than she actually was? Now, she just wanted to be left in peace to live her own life and forget the whole awful episode.

In the steaming hot bathroom she shuddered, ducked

her head under the water and massaged in the shampoo. No, what she wanted most to do was dry her hair and put on some make-up. She knew that her mum had kept some of her old clothes, so she should be able to find something clean to wear. She'd go out and enjoy her freedom, maybe go for a walk around Willesden, or follow her father's example and have a bus ride.

'Never explain' was a good way to live, she decided, getting out of the bath. It would be far easier for all concerned if no one knew where she had been these past few days.

Picking up the disgusting black and white dress, she rolled it into a ball, determined to drop it into the first litter bin she came to.

He wouldn't tell anyone, Carl decided, falling asleep as soon as he got into bed and sleeping soundly all night.

No dreams came, there were no sudden awakenings to horrid realisation, no remembering in the warm darkness what had happened. When he'd got in the previous night, Nicola had brought him a glass of water and some sort of hot drink, but he hadn't touched either of them. When he woke, he had no idea of the time except that it must be morning, maybe very early morning, though it might have been light for hours.

The silence was broken by the ringing of the doorbell, Dermot's bell, as audible down here as in the upstairs flat. He wouldn't answer it; he was sure he couldn't speak of Dermot, might never speak of him again. The bell rang once more, and this time Nicola went to the door. She had left the bedroom door open, so he could hear what she said.

'He lives in the top flat. You should go upstairs and ring at the door that's facing you.'

It must be the police. Of course. Someone had found Dermot's body, established where he lived, and had come here to ask about him, to tell his wife or girlfriend or parents or whichever of his people lived in Falcon Mews. Carl heard their feet on the stairs, then Dermot's doorbell ringing, and turned over to bury his face in the pillow. He remembered a favourite saying of Dermot's that was supposed to be funny: 'No answer was the stern reply.'

Nicola had a very clear, rather beautiful speaking voice, and he heard her telling the police officers that Dermot might have gone early to work, told them about the pet clinic and where it was. There was some conversation, Nicola said, 'Oh, no!' and he knew they must have told her Dermot was dead.

They left. He heard the front door close, and Nicola came into the bedroom.

'I heard,' he said, his voice sounding dulled and broken as anyone would say it should have done.

'They don't know how it happened. Or they didn't say. They didn't say anything about foul play. That's the term, isn't it?'

'Newspapers' term, I expect.'

'He was found in Jerome Crescent. It's a shock, I must

say. Sudden death is always a shock, isn't it, even if you didn't much like the dead person. I must go to work now, but I expect they'll come back, they'll want to search the place, or they will if his death was suspicious. You'll talk to them? You know more about Dermot than anyone, I should think.'

He listened to her going, her high heels on the stairs, the pause while she picked up her bag, the creak the front door made and the click as she closed it as softly as she could behind her.

It must be Monday morning, Carl supposed. He got up and walked into the shower, not waiting for the water to heat up but stepping into it and shivering at its cold touch. Jeans, sweatshirt, trainers. All much as usual, though it wasn't as usual, was it? Eating was impossible. He would never eat anything again. Stretched out on his father's sofa, he wondered why he always thought of this piece of furniture as Dad's. Almost everything in the house had been his father's, yet he never thought of the tables and chairs and beds as his, only this sofa. The police would know by now that Dermot had been killed, that his death had not been an accident. 'Murdered' why don't you say? he thought. You mustn't say it, though, when they come and talk to you. You must just answer what they ask.

His throat was parched and his mouth dry, no matter how much water he drank. There must be some reason for that but he didn't know what it was. He waited a long time for the police. Perhaps they would never come. Perhaps they thought Dermot had been killed in a road accident and they were searching for the driver of the car that hit him. Such a thing could hardly happen in narrow, bendy Jerome Crescent.

The police arrived at ten to one, when Carl had almost given them up. He had to tell himself as he was walking towards the front door not to speak to them unless they spoke to him, not to express any opinions about Dermot, not to ask questions; above all, not to speak of murder, or of Dermot as 'the murdered man'.

They told him rather baldly what had happened. They asked only one question, and that was whether they could go into Dermot's flat. No reason was given. If he were an innocent man, nothing more than Dermot's landlord, would he ask if they had seen Miss Soames? Did they know he had a fiancée? Did she know what had happened? Oh yes, they would take care of notifying her, said the older man. Carl gave them a key and they went upstairs.

Carl hadn't given a thought to Sybil until now. Picturing her hearing the news, understanding that the man she was going to marry had been killed in the street, more or less outside her own home, would be what the newspapers would call 'a devastating blow'. Poor Sybil. Perhaps she had loved Dermot, been in love with him, and now this had happened. Don't be a fool, Carl told himself. Pull yourself together.

The police came back downstairs. The younger one was carrying a briefcase, and it seemed to Carl to have more in it than when they had gone up. Papers, certificates, records of something or other? Of no interest to him, nothing to do with him, nothing to incriminate him.

The older one said it might be helpful to have his phone number in case they needed to get in touch, and Carl gave it to him. He saw them out, went into the living room and sat down. From what he had read and seen, he might have expected them to ask where he had been the previous evening, but they hadn't asked. They must believe that the only connection between him and Dermot was the usual relationship between landlord and tenant: remote, a matter of business – one paid the rent, the other received it. Of course it hadn't been like that, but how would they know?

Lying on the sofa in the living room, he had nothing to do, almost nothing to think about. But after a time, his mind filled with scenes of the previous evening, of the dark waters of the canal and his backpack floating, then sinking with that queer sucking sound, and of the fat, round goose as green as the grass and the oak leaves, sitting on the hall table, quietly mocking him.

CHAPTER TWENTY-FIVE

Nicola came home early, just after five, bringing with her the *Evening Standard*. Carl had no desire to read the details, but he looked at the picture of Dermot – when he was alive, of course; there was no picture of him dead – and read the story to please Nicola.

She wanted to talk about what had happened, as more or less everyone in Maida Vale would now be discussing the case. Why would anyone kill Dermot? Money was the general consensus, or even to steal his phone. Was his phone missing? The newspaper didn't say. Someone with a lively imagination suggested that a former lover of Sybil Soames, jealous of this new fiancé, had done it. Several residents of Falcon Mews who had never spoken to Carl before approached him in the street when he and Nicola went out to eat, to express their amazement, disgust, horror or disbelief. What a shock it must have been for him and the young lady, said Mr Kaleejah, walking his dog for the third time that day. Nothing like this had ever happened before in the vicinity of Elgin Avenue, said someone else. That it hadn't been anywhere near Elgin Avenue, Carl didn't say. He smiled and nodded. Nicola shook her head and thanked them for their concern.

They walked to the Canal Café on the Edgware Road and ate fish and chips and drank lager. Soon, thought Carl, when I find a new tenant, I'll have money to pay for things myself.

Two days passed and the police didn't return. Nor did they phone. The only caller was Sybil. Carl wasn't particularly surprised by this visit, though he hadn't exactly expected to see her. What astonished him was her appearance. She was dressed in deep mourning: long black skirt, big black shoulder bag, high-necked black blouse and black jacket, her head wrapped in a black scarf like a Muslim woman. He knew he ought to say how sorry he was for her loss, and he did say it, hesitating over the words, almost stammering.

She came into the hallway, saying, 'Yes, it's been terrible for me. I shall never get over it.'

He thought he should ask her to sit down, offer her something to drink, remembering that she wouldn't touch alcohol. But the need to offer her a seat and a glass of orange juice failed to arise as she walked straight upstairs and, with the key Dermot must have given her, let herself into the top flat. She had come for some of her things she had left behind, Carl supposed. Nothing could be more likely, seeing that she had spent day after day here with Dermot. And sure enough, after about ten minutes she came back down the stairs, the black bag stuffed with what appeared to be heavy objects. Opening the door, she said to him – oddly, he thought – that he hadn't seen the last of her.

Carl couldn't help thinking that her words might have been Dermot's.

L izzie had managed to pass the whole day of her return without telling her parents about her abduction, and she was sure she had done the right thing. Now she had to figure out what to tell the school where she worked. She probably no longer had a job. She didn't much care. There was no way she could tell them the truth.

She phoned Stacey's apartment in Pinetree Court on the landline. The phone was answered by Elizabeth Weatherspoon. Had she already moved in? When Lizzie asked if she could come round and collect her handbag, which she had left there some days previously, Elizabeth said it was with the concierge. If Lizzie wanted it – she spoke as if the matter was in doubt – she could pick it up from his office.

Lizzie got a very cool reception from the concierge, but she also got the bag. Her phone was still in it, and the key to her own flat, and possibly what money she had, though she couldn't remember how much this should be.

She returned to the flat in Iverson Road, and while she was resolving not to go near her parents until she absolutely had to, in case they asked her more questions about her disappearance, her mother phoned. Eddy next door, as he was usually referred to by the Milsoms, had a virus and was bedbound. The pug too was ill and his mother wanted it taken to the vet.

'Why doesn't she take it then?'

'She says she can't leave Eddy.'

'He's not a baby, he's a grown man,' said Lizzie.

'It's not what I say, it's what she says. Your father's gone somewhere on the number seven bus, and I've got an appointment with the dentist.'

'Tell me you're not expecting me to take the bloody dog to the vet?'

'That silly Eddy's in an awful state. Eva said he was crying.'

So Lizzie got on the number 6 bus and, with an ill grace, picked up Brutus the pug from her parents' neighbours. 'I've made an appointment with someone. I don't know who, since the tragedy, but it'll be all right,' said Eddy's mother.

Lizzie didn't know what she was talking about.

'I won't ask you in to see Eddy in case he's infectious. I've booked a taxi for you and Brutus.'

The taxi came and Lizzie got in with the dog in a rather grand basket.

At the Sutherland Pet Clinic, Melissa the vet was sitting at the reception desk, looking harassed.

'Where's the man who used to work here?' Lizzie asked.

'Dermot?' said Melissa. 'Didn't you know? It was a shocking thing: he was murdered.'

Lizzie didn't know what to say.

'It's awful, isn't it?' Melissa continued. 'It seems callous to talk about it so soon, but we're desperate for someone to take his place. If you hear of anyone, you'll let us know, won't you?'

Melissa took Brutus into the surgery and Lizzie waited in reception. It wasn't her first visit to the clinic – she had of course been there before to talk to Dermot and get hold of the Weatherspoons' phone number, but on that occasion she had taken little notice of the room. It was rather nice, she thought now, quiet, and different from what she would have expected in that it didn't smell of dog. The swivel chair drawn up to the counter and the computer she was already familiar with. There was one of those water dispensers in the corner of the room, surely for people, not dogs. Up on the wall was a photograph of the current Pet of the Month, a Great Dane who had jumped into the Regent's Park lake to rescue a child's teddy bear. Quite a pleasant place to work, thought Lizzie, not to be compared to running around for half the afternoon after a bunch of five-year-olds, which she seriously didn't want to do any more.

Melissa came back with Brutus and told Lizzie she had given him antibiotics and to keep him warm.

'This job,' said Lizzie. 'I mean the job that Dermot had . . .' She hesitated. 'I mean, I don't want to be pushy, but could I have it?'

'Well, I don't know. I don't know what Caroline would say.'

Lying came naturally to Lizzie. 'I've had two jobs

working as a veterinarian's receptionist, one in London and the other in . . .' she thought rapidly, 'Peterborough. I know all about it.'

'Could you come back at three? Caroline will be free then to talk to you.'

Lizzie phoned for a taxi, planning the reference she would have to forge, signing it with a name she could easily get off the internet. How on earth did people manage to live at all in the days before the World Wide Web?

She went back to the clinic at three, walking from Iverson Road. Not having written it down, she had forgotten the name of the place she had said she had worked at – somewhere beginning with a P, she thought. Portsmouth, Pontypridd, Penge? Never mind, Caroline didn't care and didn't ask. She read the letter of recommendation Lizzie had forged and asked her when she could start. Lizzie said how about tomorrow? So much for the school and having to fabricate excuses for her absence.

Walking home, she met her father getting off a bus and told him that the pet clinic had head-hunted her.

Head-hunted women don't need their fathers to pay half their rent, Tom thought hopefully. But Lizzie said nothing about financial independence, only that she'd had a long day and needed to put her feet up.

CHAPTER TWENTY-SIX

I n the days following the murder, Carl thought of almost nothing else. Only a psychopath or a hitman or perhaps a soldier in battle could kill someone and put the killing out of his mind. He had hated Dermot but just the same found it impossible to be sanguine about the murder. A much more satisfactory solution to the problem would have been Dermot's removing himself to a different address, or his getting married and buying a flat somewhere with Sybil. Carl found himself close to resenting the fact that he had brought his death on himself by his stupid inverted blackmail. A strange thought it was, that Dermot had directly courted murder by refusing to pay his rent.

But he still couldn't stop thinking about it all the time and every day. Nicola, who knew the murder preyed on his mind, told him he must get over it.

'You're not involved,' she said. 'I wouldn't say you ought to be glad. Of course not. But it has taken a weight off your mind. It's removed a worry.'

'I wouldn't want to think like that,' he said, conscious

of outrageous hypocrisy. 'It must be wrong in anyone's philosophy to feel relief at someone's death, especially death by violence.'

That night he had the first of his dreams. He could hear a moaning from upstairs that grew in volume and suddenly broke off. He climbed the stairs and it was a slow climb, his steps made sluggish by some unseen force, but he reached the top at last and made his way into the living room. All was silent. Dermot lay on the floor, his face and head a bloody mass of torn flesh and broken bones. Carl tried to cry out, but only a whimpering sound came. He was sitting up in bed when he woke and the whimpering went on. Nicola was asking him what was wrong. He didn't answer her.

He forced himself to lie down and breathe steadily. She reached out and took hold of his hand. He thought, I killed someone. I murdered a man. That's something that will never go away. It will be with me for ever, for the rest of my life and beyond, if there is a beyond. Nothing I can do will ever get rid of it, because I did it and it is written in my past.

Dermot's funeral took place at one of the churches he had attended. The first Carl knew of it was when Sybil brought two older women to the house and rang the doorbell.

'I could have let us in,' she said. 'I've got Carl's key, but I didn't want to be rude.'

She didn't introduce the women. The one that looked

a lot like Dermot said, 'Pleased to meet you. I'm Dermot's mum and this is his auntie. I should say, I *was* his mum. We'll go upstairs and help clean out his clothes and bits and pieces if you've no objection.'

They were exactly as Carl would have expected Dermot's mother and aunt to be, both short and squat, wearing black straw hats and black coats. Sybil was dressed in the same black clothes she had worn when she called round last time; no hat, but a black headscarf tied under her chin. They went upstairs and stayed there for over an hour.

It was impossible for Carl to relax while they were in the house, but was relaxation ever to be thought of now? He faced the horrible truth that the mother of the man he had murdered was in his house, was upstairs. It was both unbelievable and true. He had returned to pacing, to walking up and down, opening doors and closing them, sitting down and getting up and pacing again, the way he had done when he first realised how Dermot intended to withhold the rent.

When they came down, should he make them tea, or at least offer it? he wondered. The thought of sitting down with them and talking about Dermot – what else could they talk about? – was so dreadful that he gasped aloud. He went out into the hall when he heard their feet on the stairs. They were all carrying bags that must have been Dermot's, and the bags were stuffed full of the bits and pieces Dermot's mother had talked about. Carl wondered if much of it was his property, as almost all the furnishing of the flat had been, all of it inherited from his father. But he didn't care.

Dermot's mother expressed his own desire precisely. 'We'll go and leave you in peace.'

The aunt said, 'It was nice to meet you,' and Sybil, nodding as if to confirm this meaningless statement, added, 'See you soon.'

From the window he watched them make their way along Falcon Mews in the direction of the tube station, or perhaps a bus. They had shown no overt grief, no horror at what had happened, only a dull acceptance. Carl felt sick. He asked himself if there would be any further developments, any more visits, police inquiries, relatives or friends of Dermot turning up. If so, it must be faced, and it was nothing compared to what he had been through these past months.

You're free now, he told himself, You didn't mean to kill him, not at first, and when you did, no one saw you or connected you with his death. It's all over. Hold on to that.

Nicola came home earlier than usual, carrying two bags full of food: a roast chicken, a selection of cheeses from the local delicatessen, white grapes, a mango and a large pineapple and the ingredients for a special kind of salad. The wine she had bought was being sent, she said, but for one bottle of rosé, which she had with her.

'I'll soon have money,' Carl said. 'Just wait a couple of weeks and then I'll advertise the flat. There's such a demand round here that it'll go at once.'

She put her arms round him. 'There's no hurry, sweetheart. Wait a little. It will look rather . . . well, not like you or me, come to that . . . grasping. We could go away somewhere first. You're in need of a holiday and I've got a couple of weeks owing.'

He wanted to tell her not to remind him he had no work and no money, but he restrained himself. Maybe he could start writing again soon. 'We'll see,' he said. 'What I'd like to do would be to go out to eat – to celebrate.'

She pulled away, and stared at him. 'Celebrate what?'

'I don't know why I said that. I wasn't thinking.' He started to tell her about the visit that afternoon of Dermot's mother and aunt. 'I think they live up north somewhere. They were going to take huge carrier bags full of bric-a-brac on the train.'

'I'm sure you were nice to them, Carl,' she said, but her tone was that of someone who believed the reverse was true.

It was scarcely a quarrel, but it left him feeling sore and resentful. Nicola put away the food and drink she had bought and opened the wine, still cold from the chill cabinet of the shop. They sat side by side on the sofa and she said, 'Let's go to one of those boat cafés on the canal. That wouldn't trouble your conscience so much because they're cheap.'

The phone rang. He knew it must be his mother because no one else used the landline. Her astonishment and horror at Dermot's murder had already been voiced. This time she wanted to tell him about his grandmother's shingles. Carl made appropriate noises.

'Now, darling, the most important thing: I've got a tenant for your flat. Aren't I clever? An estate agent, that's me, and I don't charge a fee.'

193

'No, Mum, not yet, it's too soon. I mean, thanks, it's brilliant, but I don't want to let it yet.'

'But why not, darling? You're in need of the rent, aren't you? You told me you were.'

'Of course I am. But I can wait a few weeks. You haven't told this person they can have it, have you?'

'No, of course not. And by the way, it's horrible the way you use a plural when you mean a singular. It's not just you, it's everyone under thirty, and a lot over.'

Carl said, 'Sorry, Mum. I'll try not to, but I can't promise.'

Nicola asked what that was about. He told her. 'You were quite right to say no. Let's go out, shall we?'

They had another glass of the rosé first. Nicola's approval was nice, but still he asked himself why he had turned down his mother's offer.

'Why was I right to say no?' he asked Nicola as they walked down the mews. 'I'm beginning to think I shouldn't have.'

'It shows respect for Dermot. I know he treated you badly, but he had such a horrible death. Any decent person would feel pity and – well, indignation. You didn't want another tenant in there yet; you wanted to wait.'

Carl said nothing. It really didn't matter if he waited, say, a couple of weeks.

There was no sign of Sybil the next day. Carl hoped that she might have gone away on holiday with her parents, although the season appeared to be over, and most people were back at work.

While Nicola was having a shower in his bathroom, he went upstairs to use the bathroom that had been Dermot's and found the place full of what Sybil would call 'toiletries'. These bottles and jars were the sort that came from back-street pharmacies or the soap and shampoo department of a supermarket. She might not want them but she need not think she could dump them on him. He was thinking how he must tell her to take them away when he realised he had no phone number for her, and although he knew where she lived, no email or postal address.

Just as he was deciding he must go to Jerome Crescent and put a note through her door, he heard her footsteps on the stairs. But now that his chance had come, he felt rather awkward telling her he had had a shower in the bathroom that had been Dermot's. He waited, listening, and when he heard her leave, he felt sure she wouldn't come back again. She would have completed whatever tasks had brought her back to Dermot's rooms. He went upstairs and found the bathroom just as it had been. Full of her things. What did it really matter that a few jars of bath oil and sachets of cheap shampoo were left behind? Leave it a day or two and then he would throw them all away.

Carl found that he was becoming acutely aware of Sybil's presence, though he didn't know how. On Saturday evening, Nicola asked him how he knew Sybil was in the house, and he couldn't tell her, he just knew. Nicola had heard nothing. She conceded he had been right when she saw Sybil walking down the mews next morning on her way to church, prayer book in hand. She had clearly spent the night upstairs. It was another fine, sunny day, and Carl and Nicola went to Hampstead Heath, Carl painfully conscious that every item of food and every drop of drink they bought was still purchased with Nicola's money.

That kind of one-sided spending looked like coming to an end on Monday morning, however, when the post brought a letter from Carl's agent telling him that a short story he had written three years before, and forgotten about, was to be read on radio, for which he would be paid a hundred pounds.

Susanna apologised for the smallness of the sum, but it felt like a fortune to Carl. Income from his writing, recognition of his talent! A happy start to the day, it seemed, not to be spoilt by the sound of Sybil's feet in heavy shoes marching about on the top floor. So she hadn't gone. She had spent two nights up there. It was time to tell her to leave, and take her pots and jars with her. He went upstairs and knocked on the door.

She looked at him, unsmiling, as if she had never seen him before. He noticed that it wasn't shoes she was wearing, but heavy brown leather boots.

'What was it you wanted?'

Not to be left on the doorstep, he thought. 'Can I come in?'

'If you want.'

He stepped over the threshold. She left the door open.

She was still in the mourning clothes that were perhaps to become a permanency.

'I'd like you to take your things out of the bathroom,' he said. 'When you go home.'

'I'm going out now. I've got to go to work.'

'Yes, of course. But later on you must come back here and take your stuff.'

She nodded, a meaningless gesture. 'Dermot told me when we first started courting that we would live here together.'

Courting: it was the word that shocked him rather than the content of what she said. He had never before heard anyone actually use it.

'Yes, it's very sad what happened. I'll see you later,' he said.

From his front window he watched her go. There was in her walk a familiarity with her surroundings that made her look as if she had lived here all her life. He realised he didn't know where she worked or what she did: why should he know or care? She would be gone by the end of today and he would never have to see her again.

Sybil returned from work before Nicola did. Carl wouldn't have known this if he hadn't been watching for her. He went out into the hall just as she had her heavily booted right foot on the lowest stair.

'Sybil?' Had he ever before called her by what she would no doubt refer to as her Christian name? 'You'll be going home this evening, I assume. Don't forget to take your stuff from the bathroom.'

In a calm, straightforward tone she said, 'This is my home. This is where I live.'

'No, no.' Nervous as he was, he had to treat her as if she were simple. That was a word his father had used, and one that pre-dated political correctness. 'You live with your parents in Jerome Crescent. Now give me my key. You won't need it again.'

'I live here,' she said. 'I must go up now. I've things to see to.'

'No, Sybil. I'm very sorry about Dermot, but I shall have a new tenant coming in. That's why you need to go. That's why I need the key.'

'I'm the new tenant,' she said. 'I told you Dermot said I was to live here.' Suddenly her voice took on the tone of an ordinary, determined woman who knew exactly what she was doing and saying. 'I have to hold on to the key. I'm taking over my fiancé's tenancy.'

He said nothing. To think that he had believed her naïve, an ignorant fool. He went into the bathroom and threw up. Because he had eaten nothing all day, he vomited only yellow liquid.

He was still in the bathroom when Nicola came home. He had reached a stage where he had to remind himself that she didn't know he had killed Dermot. Sometimes, when he thought about it, he seemed to remember telling her, and her forgiving him or overlooking it or something.

She doesn't know. Hold on to that, he told himself. But I can tell her about Sybil, what Sybil said. I must ask her what to do. 'Sybil is here,' he said. 'She says she's the new tenant. She won't give me the key.'

'She must. Tell her you'll get the police to put her out.'

'I couldn't do that.'

'Then I will.'

'No.' The idea of the police coming meant only one thing to him: Dermot's murder. They would be in the house and they would know what had happened to the previous tenant. They would become suspicious. 'No, Nic. We can't do that. Would it be too bad to have her as the new tenant? I mean, she'd be steady and quiet and regular in her habits – I know I sound like an old-time landlady – and she wouldn't make trouble.'

'I'm not hearing this,' Nicola said.

'Yes, you are, you are. I'm saying let's have Sybil as the new tenant. It would make things easy. There'd be money coming in. She'd be on her own. She wouldn't bring men home.'

'What's happened to you, Carl? You're young. You don't talk and think like that.' In a scathing tone she said, *'She wouldn't bring men home. She wouldn't make trouble, she'd be quiet and steady.'* She didn't wait for his defence. 'What's got into you? You have to turn her out, and do it now. She can go back to her parents. I don't want her here. We'll find someone else.'

He spoke to her in a tone he had never thought possible. 'This is my house. I decide about tenants, not you.'

She didn't argue. Her face went white. 'I'm sorry,' she said. 'Let her stay. I just hope you won't regret it.'

She had said 'you', not 'we'. Whatever happens now, Carl thought, this is the beginning of the end for us.

CHAPTER TWENTY-SEVEN

Most of the pet-owners at the clinic accepted Lizzie without question. One of the few exceptions was Yvonne Weatherspoon, who had known her when she'd been a friend of Stacey. Yvonne hadn't much liked Lizzie then, and she didn't seem to like her now.

'Where's Dermot?' she asked.

Lizzie didn't know what to say. Surely Yvonne knew? It had been all over the papers and even on the London regional news. 'Didn't you see it on TV?'

'What do you mean, on TV?'

'Well, he was murdered. It was on TV and in all the papers. They still haven't got anyone for it.'

'I saw about *that* Dermot,' said Yvonne, 'but I didn't connect it with *our* Dermot. My God, what a dreadful thing. I'm really shocked.' She pointed to the occupant of the cat box. 'Sophie knows. You can tell, can't you? It's been a shock to her as well, poor angel.' She mouthed kisses to the cat through the bars of the carrier. 'A nasty animal from down the hill has scratched her and I think it's got infected. I do hope Caroline can see her. I think she's got a temperature.'

Caroline could see her this time and would keep her in to operate on the abscess. Perhaps Mrs Weatherspoon would like to leave her here and come back for her at four? 'Like' was not the word, but Yvonne had to agree.

They closed the clinic for an hour at lunchtime and Lizzie went across the street to the Sutherland Café for a sandwich and a Diet Coke. She still found it hard to sit quietly on her own. Her mind played nasty tricks, returning to the horrific days she so much wanted to forget.

When she'd first got home, she had thought about phoning Swithin Campbell and confronting him with her suspicions that he'd been in cahoots with Scotty and Redhead. But what would happen if he turned out to be dangerous? It might be better to leave things as they were, with Scotty and Redhead as far away from her as possible.

If only she had someone clever to advise her.

B ack at the pet clinic, nothing much happened until four o'clock. In the operating theatre, a small room in the back, Caroline lanced Sophie's abscess and laid her comfortably in her cat carrier to sleep until Yvonne Weatherspoon came for her. But at five past four it was Yvonne's son who called at the clinic.

'Hi, Gervaise,' said Lizzie. She was surprised and pleased to see him. He must have cancelled his trip to

Cambodia or wherever it was. Or perhaps he just hadn't left yet.

'Well, if it isn't little Lizzie,' said Gervaise Weatherspoon. 'What are you doing here?'

'I work here.'

'Do you really? My mother didn't say.' Caroline came out with the cat, still asleep in her carrier. 'Can I pay with a credit card?'

'Sure you can. That'll be a hundred and eighty pounds.'

'I'll have to get that back from my mum,' he said, and looked at Lizzie again. 'Lizzie, I owe you an apology.'

'Do you? Whatever for?'

He slipped his card into the machine. 'Last time I saw you, I said you could stay in Stacey's flat while I was away. But then my sister wanted to live there, and you must have had to move out.'

'I did,' said Lizzie. 'But that's all in the past now.' What he'd said had given her an idea. 'Can I ask you something?'

'Sure you can.'

'I need some advice.'

Gervaise looked interested, as Lizzie had thought he might. 'OK,' he said. 'Shall we meet in the café opposite after you finish here? Let me get this animal home first.'

Next morning Carl watched Sybil in the garden before she went to work, pulling up the few weeds she had allowed to take root there, cutting off the dead heads from flowers he didn't know the names of.

She probably worked as someone's cleaner, he thought. That was what she looked like. Perhaps she would clean for him. Maybe she could do decorating as well as gardening. It began to appear as if he had done rather well in not getting rid of her.

He must get her a rent book, something he had never done for Dermot. It would be more businesslike. He'd draw up another contract and have Nicola witness it. He had hoped to raise the rent this time, but now he realised he could hardly do that. Sybil wouldn't earn that much; maybe ten pounds an hour was what he had heard cleaners' wages amounted to. No, keep the rent to what Dermot had paid — or hadn't paid in recent months.

He sat down at the laptop and contrived a sort of contract for Sybil Soames to pay Carl Martin one thousand, two hundred pounds per calendar month — a good touch that, calendar month — for a one-bedroom apartment at 11 Falcon Mews, London W9. He'd arrange the signing down here in his living room. When Nicola came home from work, she usually went straight upstairs to their bedroom to change into jeans and a T-shirt, and it was after that that he and Sybil would sign the document.

He asked himself why he was treating the process with such weight and formality. Dermot's contract had never been handled like this. His mother had told him he could now get much more than twelve hundred a month, but he had said no, and she had supposed he was being generous, that asking more would be greedy. No one could know — no one would ever know — that he shuddered whenever he thought of profiting from the death of a man he had murdered.

Sybil came back at five. Her shoes made a flapping sound as she walked upstairs. A bit less than an hour later Nicola arrived, carrying a basket of strawberries, a carton of cream and a bunch of pink and purple flowers she said were zinnias. Carl showed her the contract.

She nodded. 'You're still going through with this, then?'

'You agreed it was a good idea.'

'I don't think so, Carl. As you said, it wasn't for me to agree or disagree. It's your house.'

'Well, will you witness Sybil and me signing this contract?'

'If that's what you want.'

She went up to their bedroom to change. The beginning of the end for them, he had thought their argument was. But it had passed and perhaps the end wouldn't happen. He hoped not. He picked up the phone and called Dermot's number. He couldn't yet think of it as Sybil's.

'Can't you come up here?' she said.

'I suppose so. If you like.'

Passing his bedroom door on the way, he called out to Nicola that he would want her up in Sybil's flat in a few minutes and would shout for her. It was a hot day, and a thick, humid warmth had risen to the landing. Sweat broke out on his face, on his upper lip, as he climbed the stairs. He had a strong, quite unreasonable feeling of impending doom.

Sybil opened the door before he got there and was

standing just inside. She was wearing a pale pink dress with blue and green geometric shapes all over it, which left her arms and shoulders bare.

'It's very hot up here,' he said when he was in the even more stifling atmosphere of the living room. 'Don't you want to open the windows?'

'I never open windows,' she said. 'It lets insects in.'

By now, he was bathed in sweat. 'May I sit down?'

'Be my guest,' she said.

Ridiculous, he thought. I *am* her guest. He unfolded the sheet of paper on which he had typed the contract and laid it on the round table. She remained standing. 'I have the rent contract. Would you like to read it?'

She didn't sit down, but just glanced at the contract. 'I don't need to read it. I told you I'm living here. Dermot said I should.'

'Yes, perhaps. But you still have to pay me rent.'

She shook her head vigorously. 'I don't pay rent. Why should I? I already said I'm living here.'

The perspiration was dripping down his face like tears. 'I don't think you understand. If you have rooms in someone else's property, you have to pay for it. You have to pay by the week or month. That's what this paper is about. I'll call Nicola in to witness it, if you know what that means, and then you sign and I sign and she sees us do that and she signs. OK?'

'No,' she said. 'It's not OK. I haven't got the money. I work in Lidl on the checkout.'

'Well, I'm sorry, but that means you'll have to go. You can't stay here without paying rent.'

That awful shaking of the head began again. 'I'm staying here like Dermot did. He never paid rent, not a penny, and I'm not either. This is my home now.'

'No, it's not, Sybil. If you don't go, I shall have to fetch the police to put you out.'

She took a step towards him and a cunning look spread across her face. There was deceit in it, and a half-smile. 'I saw you hit Dermot with that bag you carry,' she said. 'It must have had something heavy in it. I was in my bedroom and I saw you from the window. He just lay there. I went to bed. He was still there in the morning. I went out there at five and saw him. You killed him like a killer on TV.'

Carl stared at her.

'I'll tell the police if you make me leave. I didn't go to them before as I've always wanted somewhere to live that's not with my parents, but couldn't afford it. Now I have this place, and I don't have to pay any rent at all.'

An analogy people made when something bad had happened was to say it was a nightmare. Carl was somewhere worse than a nightmare, a conjuring of horror only bearable if he knew he would wake up. He lacked the strength to speak and she saw this. She was watching him closely, not quite with a smile but with a calm, satisfied look.

'I'll keep it nice,' she said. 'I'll pay for the electric and the gas, no need to worry about that. And I'll do the garden for free, it won't cost you.'

Still Carl couldn't speak. He got up and walked out, stumbling a little. Nicola was downstairs, doing something in the kitchen, preparing a meal perhaps. The flowers she had bought were in a vase on the windowsill, pink and mauve stiff-petalled daisies. In films when someone was in a rage or despair or the kind of situation Carl was in now, he – it was always a man – would pick up the vase of flowers and smash it against the wall. Carl stared at the vase, then lay down on the floor and buried his face in his hands. Nicola came in with the strawberries in a bowl and a jug of cream.

'Oh, Carl, sweetheart, what's wrong?'

He lifted his head, then struggled to his feet. He couldn't tell her. He couldn't tell her he was a murderer. He couldn't tell her anything.

CHAPTER TWENTY-EIGHT

I t was still warm outside when Lizzie left the clinic, and people were sitting at the tables outside the café, Gervaise among them. She sat down next to him.

'What would you like? Coffee? Tea?' he asked.

'Do you think they have – well, alcohol?'

'In this country,' he said, 'I doubt if there's anywhere they don't.'

They did. She asked for white wine, not particular about what sort. His having a cup of tea seemed to her a reproach. She would have much preferred him to have wine too.

'You wanted to ask my advice,' he said. 'What about?'

'Well, it happened a week ago but I haven't said a word to anyone. I nearly told my parents and then I thought they'd tell the police and the police would ask me questions – the sort of questions I shouldn't want to answer.'

'What would those sort of questions be, then?'

'Oh, well, never mind. Nothing important. Shall I tell you what happened?'

'That's the point of all this, isn't it?'

She began to tell him the story, starting with her meeting the so-called Swithin Campbell and his arrangement to call for her while she was staying in Pinetree Court. She told him she was sure Swithin had thought she was rich, and had put Scotty and Redhead up to abducting her.

'Didn't your mother tell you that a man called her to demand a ransom for her daughter?' she asked.

'Should she have told me?' He looked almost amused.

'I thought she might, but they got it wrong. We are both called Elizabeth, you see, and they thought I was the rich one. They took me to various places, handcuffed me and put a gag on my mouth. I don't know where I was, it was nowhere I knew. They fed me on bread and water like in a prison, they moved me about and took me down to south London. It was while I was there that a beautiful enormous pigeon flew into the window and smashed a pane, and the horrible men who were holding me ran away and left me. I suppose they believed it was the police breaking in. I got out and got a taxi back to my parents. There, now you know.'

Lizzie took a large and satisfying draught of her wine. The girl who had served them had brought two chocolates on a glass dish to go with their drinks, and she took one. 'What do you think I should do?'

'I remember when we were children and your parents lived near Stacey's parents in Willesden. Do you remember that?' he asked.

'Of course I do, but what's it got to do with anything?'

'You used to come round to Stacey's to play, and you used to tell the most enormous whoppers. That's the name they gave to lies in those days. Do you remember that too?'

'I don't know what you mean.'

'Yes you do, Lizzie. I was visiting once and your dad came to fetch you, and I heard him ask Stacey's mother, like it was a sort of joke, if you'd, I quote, been up to your usual tricks of telling porkies. There are a lot of words in the English language for telling lies.'

'I wasn't telling lies. Not now. It's all true,' said Lizzie, remembering how afraid she'd been.

'Anyone who didn't know you,' said Gervaise, 'might believe that tale, especially if you left out the bit about the miraculous bird.' He paused, and smiled at her. 'Just a piece of advice. After all, that's what you asked for. Next time you tell that story, leave out the bird.' He went inside to pay the bill.

Lizzie got up and walked in the other direction, up to Maida Vale. She'd never liked that family; it wasn't just Yvonne Weatherspoon, they were all the same. To be honest with herself, she had only asked Mr Clever Gervaise for advice because she fancied him.

Well, that was the end of that. If nobody would believe her, she might as well put the whole experience out of her head. It had all been a mistake, not meant for her. She had thought she might warn the other Elizabeth about those two men, but now she didn't care. Elizabeth Weatherspoon would just have to look out for herself.

Meanwhile she, Lizzie, had a date that evening with

a really nice man who'd asked her out when he brought his Basenji into the clinic. Only for a drink, but perhaps it would lead to greater things. While she waited for the number 98 bus, she thought about which of Stacey's clothes she should wear for the evening.

Tom was also on a bus – the number 18 – and also giving some thought to a serious subject. The evening before, he and Dot had been to a birthday party, his sister Wendy's, and there Wendy's next-door neighbour had listened with interest to his account of his bus rides and asked him why he didn't write a book about them. If Tom had only known, Trevor Vincent made that enquiry of everyone who talked to him at any length about any hobby or pursuit. He did so not because he cared or knew anything about the particular topic, but because he had no other conversation.

'Do you think I could?' Tom had asked.

'Have you got a computer or a tablet or whatever?'

'Of course I have. Shall I give it a go?

'You do that,' said Trevor Vincent, moving off to find his wife and go home.

Tom thought very little more about the suggestion that evening, but next day the conversation came back to him. Well, why not? Describing today's adventure might provide the opening of such a book, the incident in Harlesden High Street, for instance, when those Chinese people had refused to get off the bus when told to do so because they had no passes but only offered cash.

The driver had tried to turn them off but they had sat in the vacant seats playing some strange musical instruments Tom had never seen before. A huge burly man (not Chinese) had joined them and also refused to get off the bus when the police came and told them to. Tom had had to get off himself then, sad not to see the outcome. That could all go in his book. He might start it tomorrow.

The Basenji man, whose name was Adam Yates, took Lizzie to something more like a wine bar than a pub. He seemed quite overcome by Stacey's beautiful cream-coloured dress and jacket, though Lizzie herself thought it was a bit over the top for the Unicorn Lounge. She was very hungry, so Adam's suggestion that they have dinner in the Unicorn's rather beautiful dining area met with an enthusiastic response. Lizzie had a principle that if a restaurant, no matter how grand and expensive, had an illustrated menu – coloured photos of chicken tikka and fish pie – she would refuse to eat there. There was nothing of that sort here. The food was civilised and delicious, quite unlike that dreadful evening with the awful Swithin Campbell and his boring talk, Adam made no suggestion of coming in when he took her home, but kissed her lightly on the cheek and went to catch the 82 bus.

Next morning he phoned. He had tickets for a concert. A famous orchestra from Hungary was playing Mozart and Respighi and would she come with him on Friday?

Of course she accepted, already planning to wear the green suit with the pearls. Lizzie had never heard of Respighi, but what was Google for but to help out in situations like this?

Lizzie was the kind of person for whom designated future tasks loomed large. There was little pleasure to be anticipated in completing the task Caroline had set for her: to carry all the items that had once belonged to Dermot to Carl Martin's house in Falcon Mews. Unless, of course, Carl might invite her in. She was curious to see what his place looked like. He probably wouldn't even recognise her, it had been so long since they had seen each other in their school days. They both had been close to Stacey, of course. It wasn't very far to the mews that linked Sutherland Avenue to Castellain Road. Dermot was said to have walked it, there and back, every day, but Lizzie didn't fancy the walk at all.

While Caroline was busy removing a nail from a cocker spaniel's pad, Darren was out on a call and Melissa carrying out a routine examination of Spots the Dalmatian, Lizzie had a look inside the storage cupboard, largely to assess the weight of the late Dermot's property. A pair of sheepskin gloves, a framed photograph of a dark girl with a fat face and heavy shoulders, two broken mobile phones, an ancient bible, three box files, a hardcover London atlas, two notebooks and a box of paper fasteners all added up to considerable weight. She decided that she'd postpone the task till the following week.

CHAPTER TWENTY-NINE

S ybil's parents paid her a visit at the flat in Falcon Mews on a dreary Sunday. It was late morning, and the streets were deserted; those few people who were out carried umbrellas. It was pouring with rain, torrential rain that had begun at nine and looked as though it would continue. A worse day for rain couldn't have been thought of, for it was the second and most important day of the local carnival, and the sound of it, though a little subdued, could be heard from Falcon Mews, a throb, a beat, muffled cries and shouts and music.

Carl saw Mr and Mrs Soames arrive. He guessed who they were, for who else could they be? Mrs Soames looked very much like her daughter, or her daughter looked very much like her. They came along the mews under a single large black umbrella, which they only folded up when Sybil answered the door.

'She'll want me to meet them,' Carl said to Nicola. 'You'll see. Maybe they'll have tea first and then she'll bring them down here and present them to me.'

'Does it matter?'

'Well, insofar as nothing matters any more, no, it doesn't.'

'Carl, what's wrong? Why does nothing matter? If you don't want Sybil living here, why did you say she could?'

'I can't answer that, Nic. I will never be able to answer that. I would if I could, but you have to take it from me that it's impossible. She's here for ever or until she chooses to go.'

Nicola turned away and looked out of the window at the ceaseless rain, at Mr Kaleejah, at his dog trotting along, ignoring the water underfoot and the water descending from the low grey clouds. 'What's that dog called? Do you know?'

'I don't know and I don't give a shit.'

Nicola walked out of the room without a word.

For a while Carl had convinced himself that what he had done was not important. But gradually guilt and shame had arrived, as well as not so much a fear of discovery as a fear of some kind of retribution for his wickedness. He knew now that his action, irrespective of Dermot's own wrongdoing, would always be with him, day after day, year after year. In the unlikely, indeed impossible, event of his confessing his crime, asking for forgiveness, walking into the police station and telling whoever was there that he had killed a man, would his fear go away? When his guilt was known, when everyone knew, perhaps he would no longer be haunted by it. But it was with him now and inhabited his body like his heart did. It slept with him and woke with him, it lived with him like an organ. It would never leave.

He tried to deflect himself from this wretched reverie by thinking of practical things; for instance, getting some sort of job. He should never have set forth in life thinking he could live on his writing. He'd relied on renting out his property for his livelihood, and this was no longer possible. A tenant, and now that tenant's ghastly successor, had found a way to deprive him of his rent while enjoying all the benefits of a home in one of the best parts of London.

If Dermot knew from beyond the grave what Sybil was doing, would he be proud of her? And what could Carl do now? A philosophy degree was training for nothing. But that was the qualification he had; it must be a start. He could perhaps take a teacher training course, teach English.

Footsteps sounded heavily on the stairs and Sybil called out, 'Hi there, Carl.' She had recently stopped calling him Mr Martin. Perhaps she thought her new status as a permanent householder made her his equal. 'Can I bring my mum and dad in to make your acquaintance?'

He would have liked to tell her to go to hell, never to speak to him again, but he got up and opened the door. One thing particularly struck him about the couple at the foot of the stairs. They were nervous. Of him, or of Sybil?

'These are my mum and dad,' said Sybil. 'They're called Cliff and Carol. This is Mr Martin.'

Carol Soames said she was pleased to meet him. Cliff Soames said nothing for a moment but looked around the room apparently without approval.

'You own this place, do you?' he said, fixing Carl with a stare.

'I told you he did, Dad.'

'Let's hear what he has to say for himself. Belongs to you, does it? A young man like you?'

'Yes,' Carl said.

'Sybil says your dad left it to you. A whole house to do as you like with. That true?'

Carl hated this man's attitude. Whatever hold Sybil had over him, he wasn't obliged to take this. 'Yes, I can do with it as I like, and one of the things I'm going to do is turn you out of it. Now. Get out and take your fat wife with you.'

Immediately he said it he regretted that 'fat'. 'Go on, leave,' he continued, not touching Cliff but pushing Carol out of the room. 'Get out now. I never want to see you here again.'

They hurried out quickly, clearly in shock at Carl's anger. Sybil stared at him. 'Don't think that bothered me. I don't care if I never see them again.' She lumbered up the stairs without another word.

Nicola had heard it all, coming silently from the kitchen and standing in the doorway. 'You were very rude,' she said, 'but you managed to stop the lecture he was going to give you on capitalism versus anarchy.'

'Maybe.'

'Shall we go out, do something? It's brightening up. At any rate, the rain's stopped.'

'All right,' Carl said, still in the same gloomy, downcast tone. 'I've got no money. Where can you go and what can you do without money?'

'In a week's time you'll get the rent,' she said.

As they walked along the mews, Carl began to consider, not for the first time, what he could or should tell Nicola. But as before, there was no answer that was both a reason for no money coming in, such as Sybil's being unable to afford the rent, and, far more difficult to explain, for his tolerating this void like some sort of rich philanthropist. No one would believe such a tale, and certainly not Nicola, who knew him so well, who knew he disliked Sybil, who knew how totally strapped for cash he was.

He said to her suddenly, 'Is there anything I can do to make money quickly? I mean, get a job tomorrow or very soon that would bring me in, say, a hundred and fifty pounds a week?'

'Oh, Carl, you don't know much about wages, do you? How could you? But you don't have to. You'll get twelve hundred pounds next week.'

He would have to tell her the truth. But the truth was so terrible that he would lose her. If she wouldn't tolerate his selling a drug to Stacey, how could he expect her to accept that he had killed a man? And what would she *do* about it? Force him to go to the police? But would it take much forcing?

'Where are we going?' he asked now.

'Where would you like to go?'

'A pub,' he said. 'To have a drink, something strong. I need it.'

They went to the Carpenters' Arms in Lauderdale Road, where they met the local bookshop owner, Will Finsford, and his girlfriend Corinne. The girls kissed, delighted to see each other. It was still only midday, but Will plied them with wine that Nicola firmly and effectively, and Carl feebly and in vain, refused.

It had been several months since they had seen each other. Corinne and Will sympathised with Carl over Dermot's death as if his tenant had been a friend, and wanted to know if they had found someone new to occupy the top floor. Carl, his head feeling muzzy with alcohol already, was looking at Nicola as she spoke. There was nothing to compare to beauty like hers: those soft but classical features, those dazzling eyes, and the blondeness of her – the pale glossy hair and the slightly darker, more golden eyebrows. And more than her physical beauty, there was her essential goodness. It would all be taken from him when he told her what he had done. As he must, as he had to, in the next few days. She had left him before. Of course she had come back. But she wouldn't come back this time.

Nicola was telling the others about Sybil Soames taking over the tenancy, but she said nothing about Carl's reaction to Sybil's appearance and manner. So lovely herself, she spoke of other women as if they were equally beautiful and gentle.

When Carl's glass was empty, she took one of his hands and whispered to him that it was time to go. She had already got a promise from Corinne that she would phone to accept one of the dates Nicola had given them to come over. Outside the rain had cleared, and the sky was a cloudless blue. Carl had scarcely said a word for the past hour, but now he began on his current favourite subject, his inability to pay for anything and the shame this brought him. The shops of Sutherland Avenue and Clifton Road often had notices in their windows offering work for supermarket staff or restaurant waiters. He would have to apply for such a job. Maybe tomorrow.

They had reached the Rembrandt Gardens, overhung by broad-leaved trees. Nicola sat down on a wooden seat and motioned to him to sit beside her. The seat overlooked a part of the canal where it widened into a lake with an island in its centre clustered over by water birds. Nicola knew that Carl wouldn't take kindly to her telling him he had neither the experience nor the patience for manual work; instead, intent on cheering him up, she reminded him that next week he would have an envelope with twelve hundred pounds from Sybil.

He turned his eyes from the island and the birds and looked at her. 'I won't get it,' he said. 'It won't come. Let's go home.'

Nicola felt very near to tears. Whatever was the matter with Carl now? What did he mean about the rent not coming in? Surely Sybil would pay. Was it the book he was unable to get on with? Was it simply the presence of Sybil in his house?

It wasn't far to Falcon Mews. When they entered the house, there was no sign of Sybil and no sound from upstairs.

'Shall we have a cup of tea? I've got some of those nice biscuits you like, the round white chocolate ones.'

She made the tea, set out the white biscuits. They sat down on Dad's sofa. On the walk back, Carl had come to a decision: he would tell her that he'd killed Dermot. But sitting beside her now, looking at her, so beautiful and loving, he knew it was impossible. He couldn't even pretend it had happened by accident. There was nothing he could invent to account for lifting up that bag with its green pottery contents and bringing it down on Dermot's head.

'You were going to tell me why you fear Sybil won't pay the rent next week. You were, weren't you?' Nicola said.

'She thinks I killed Dermot and she says she'll tell the police she saw me do it if I make her pay. That's what it amounts to,' Carl said in a single breath.

Nicola looked shocked. 'She *can't*. She's out of her mind. She can't think that way. Where does she get such an idea? To suspect you of all people, a gentle person like you, of doing such a thing.'

He said nothing for a moment. He was wondering what she would say if he told her the truth.

'Of course the poor woman's mentally ill,' Nicola went on. 'But to accuse you with her insane belief? Why didn't you tell me before?'

'I don't know. But now you can see why I can't risk her going to the police with this story.'

'But it isn't true, Carl. They wouldn't believe her. You'd tell them the truth and then ask her to get out of this house. You would find someone else for the flat.'

'Nic, my sweetheart, I can't do that. Leave it now. You know what the situation is. Wait till tomorrow or Wednesday, say, and if the rent comes we'll know she's thought better of her accusation and all is well.'

But all would not be well. He knew that. Strangely, for he had always believed that telling a lie, and as monstrous a lie as this one, could never make you feel better, this one did.

CHAPTER THIRTY

On Monday – a dry day apart from the inevitable occasional showers – Tom set off on a trip to Leyton Green on the number 55. He picked it up at Oxford Circus, having got there on his favourite number 6 from Willesden. The number 55 proceeded through Holborn and Clerkenwell to Shoreditch. Tom hardly knew these places and found them shabbier than he expected, with the exception of Shoreditch, which had been much smartened up and seemingly filled with trendy shops and restaurants.

The bus might be full of schoolchildren in an hour's time, but now it was half empty. From the laughter and shouting, there appeared to be a lot of young people upstairs, but Tom never now went to the upper deck; he preferred to be downstairs at the front on the right, where his fellow travellers were mostly women and a few girls.

One young man did get on, though, as the bus moved into Hackney; or Tom thought it must be Hackney. To find his bearings when in an unfamiliar district, he usually looked at the newsagents' shopfronts or a post office or police station where lettering over the front entrances told the observer that this was Clapton News or Islington Central Post Office. But he saw no clues of that sort as the bus proceeded along wide streets and shabby narrow ones, heading for where he had no idea.

The young man who had got on at the possible beginnings of Hackney stayed downstairs and settled himself on the left-hand side in a seat next to the window. Tom had expected him to go to the upper deck, but he hadn't. He was a black-haired man, beardless and with very white skin, carrying on his back what Tom would have called a satchel. He kept it on his back as the bus went on into what a post office sign told Tom was Clapton.

At the next stop, a crowd of women and children got on and the young man got off. Most of the mothers and children went upstairs, and those who remained went to the back of the bus, where you could sit facing each other. It was then that Tom saw that the young man had left his bag behind, on the floor, pushed into the corner. It no longer looked like a simple satchel but rather more threatening – a container for something dangerous. It would be hard to say what suggested this; it might only have been that its shape gave the impression of having something heavy and metallic inside. It had a heavy metal zip that went all the way round it. Tom didn't like the look of it at all.

He went up to the driver and told him about the bag. Then he told him about the young man who had got off, leaving it behind.

'It'll go to the lost property department,' said the driver.

'Yes, but that won't be for several hours. It ought to be dealt with now.'

'I tell you what, I'll have it taken off and left in the garage when we get to Leyton Green.'

With that Tom was expected to be satisfied. But he wasn't. He admitted afterwards that he had been thinking of his own skin just as much as the children eating ice-cream cornets in the back seats of the bus, and the noisy young people upstairs. He didn't select the place where he got off with the bag; it just happened to be beside a patch of open space, where people were strolling about under the trees and someone was picking chrysanthe-mums. Tom had once told a woman to leave the flowers alone and got a mouthful of abuse.

He carried the heavy bag up to the railings and set it down on the pavement. Things happened fast after that. He was a little way away from it, back at the bus stop reading the timetable up on the post, when there came a huge blinding flash and a roar as the sinister black bag exploded.

When Tom came to, he was lying on the pavement and a woman and a small boy were beside him, both prone. The woman was bleeding, Tom couldn't see where from, only that she was alive. The boy struggled to sit up, then get to his feet. Blood was pouring from his left arm.

Tom felt for his mobile phone, but it wasn't needed; he could see three other people on their phones. Somewhere a siren was braying. It seemed to belong to an ambulance that roared to a halt at the bus stop. The paramedics tumbled out. Tom was amazed by the speed with which they had got there, and then by the arrival of a second ambulance, and one police car after another. Holding on to the bus stop pole for the support he suddenly needed, he watched the police holding the uninjured people back from the place where the bomb had gone off; the place where he'd put it. The woman and the boy with the bleeding arm were already being loaded on to stretchers. He looked away as another woman on a stretcher was covered with a white sheet that meant death.

A paramedic was telling him he must get into the proffered wheelchair and be taken to hospital when a policeman interrupted them and asked him if he had seen what had happened.

'He's a hero,' said the woman who'd been with the small boy. 'I saw him carry that bomb thing off the bus. He saved all the people on the bus.'

Tom was dreadfully embarrassed.

'Is that a fact, sir?' said the policeman.

'Well, yes. I suppose so,' said Tom. 'I'm not a hero, though. I'm going to get on the next bus.'

'Not yet,' said a paramedic. 'Your leg is bleeding and your right arm doesn't look too good. Come along, into the chair and we'll get you seen to.'

So the wheelchair was unfolded and Tom was put into it much against his will. Sitting down, he could see a wound in his knee and blood leaking from his arm. The paramedic, pushing him to the second ambulance, said, 'You were very brave. If that had gone off a couple of minutes sooner, it'd have blown you to kingdom come.'

Lifted into the ambulance, Tom looked back at the scene. Most of the people had been picked up from the pavement, but signs of them remained, blood lying in shallow pools. He wanted to go home.

CHAPTER THIRTY-ONE

'One good thing has come out of it, though,' said Dot Milsom on the phone. 'This ghastly bomb has put an end to all his junketing about on buses.'

'You ought to be proud of him.' Lizzie was still at an age to enjoy setting her parents against one another. 'He was amazing. A hero – that's what people are saying about him. Where is he now?'

'He was brought home last night. I suppose you'll come over and see him?'

'I will tomorrow. I have a dinner date tonight. Say hello to him for me.'

'I know it's trendy to say that, but wouldn't it be a lot nicer to send your love?' But Lizzie had put the phone down.

Adam Yates, her Basenji date from the clinic, had been to the Iverson Road flat several times by now. He said he liked it, and that she was lucky to have a self-contained place of her own. He himself owned a flat in Tufnell Park, and although he made little of it, he couldn't disguise its considerable size and pleasant leafy location. This evening, she thought, he would come back with her, and this time – would he stay?

In half an hour's time he was calling for her and they were going to the Tricycle Theatre, just down the road really. You didn't dress up for the Tricycle, but it wasn't jeans and Primark T-shirt wear either, so Lizzie put on her best black trousers and a white shirt with a cardigan. Reviewing her conversation with her mother, she liked the idea of inviting Adam to one of her family dinners, but first she must take all that stuff belonging to Dermot McKinnon to his old flat in Falcon Mews. Perhaps she could do it one night next week, before she went to visit her parents?

The front doorbell rang absolutely on time. No previous boyfriend had ever been so punctual. The trouble was that she still felt fearful when someone rang the bell, after what had happened with Redhead and Scotty.

As she went to answer the door, she thought, I'll tell Adam how I feel and then tell him the whole story. He won't be like Gervaise Weatherspoon; he'll believe me.

Carl slept well that night but awoke next morning to a weight of dread that shaped itself into sickness. He could eat nothing, drink nothing, not even coffee. He waited for Sybil's footsteps on the stairs, holding his breath. They sounded, a heavy clumping, and then came the front door banging with more of a crash than usual.

Nicola went to work. She'd told him she would be late

home because she was going out in the evening with two of her old flatmates, and the boyfriend of one of them. Carl had been asked but he had said no, he was sorry but he didn't feel up to it. She said goodbye to him that morning with more than usual tenderness and love, and he was sure this was due to that convincing lie he had told. Perhaps he should lie to her more? But no, there were only a few hours left if he did what he meant to do. And he must.

Sybil was asking to die as Dermot had. This was another thing the two had in common: a propensity to invite their own deaths. But this death couldn't come from the stairs or from a fall from a window. Instead, some impulse sent him up to the bathroom and the store of alternative medicine his father had accumulated.

The fifty capsules of the DNP that Stacey had not purchased were there in the front of the cabinet, and there too, behind them, was the powder-to-liquid variety in sachets. It said on the box that the sachets should be dissolved in water and then drunk down. This was what Carl was looking for. Offering Sybil the DNP powder would be no more murder than selling DNP to Stacey had been. The last thing he had wanted was to kill Stacey, but he wanted this concoction to kill Sybil.

But had Sybil read the coroner's report in the newspaper? Would she know about DNP? Probably not. Sybil didn't impress Carl as the type who would read much of any newspapers, including the tabloids.

Carl took the box of sachets down to the kitchen, opened one and dropped the contents into a glass of water. It turned bright yellow. This, he told himself, was just a trial run: now he knew how it reacted. He found a leaflet inside the box which stated that DNP was for rapid weight loss. That it was a dangerous drug, likely to cause death if taken in large quantities, was mentioned at the end in very small print. The only difficulty now, he thought, was how to get Sybil to take it.

If Nicola came upon it, she would know what it was. She must never see it. But she wouldn't be home this evening before about ten, and by that time the deed could be done. Sybil would arrive home between five thirty and six and he must catch her in the hallway and make some friendly overture to her, using Nicola's absence as his reason for such unlikely behaviour on his part.

At lunchtime he went out. Nicola had left him some money, a twenty-pound note, and although he knew she had meant it for food, he spent it on two bottles of wine and fed himself from the fridge, bread that he toasted and the end of a piece of cheese. Before Sybil was due home, he placed a couple of DNP sachets on the hall table on top of the leaflet on which he stood the glass he had used. She came in at ten minutes to six, and ten minutes later he found her standing over the table, reading the leaflet. His heart thumped.

'I'm glad I've caught you,' he said. 'I wanted to ask you in for a drink; it doesn't have to be alcohol. Nicola's away for the evening, you see, and I wanted some company.'

She looked him in the face, puzzled. 'Well, OK, I don't mind.'

'I thought it would be a good idea for us to try to be friends. I know we haven't been on very good terms, but that ought to change, don't you think?'

Astonishingly, she seemed to believe him. 'I'll just go up and leave my stuff,' she said.

He went back into the living room, but came out after a minute to see if she had taken the sachets on the table. She hadn't. Would she ask him about them? He could only wait and see.

She returned more quickly than he expected, having changed her T-shirt and cardigan for a fussy pink blouse with a frill round the neck and her boots for court shoes from which her feet bulged. Was she trying to look attractive for him? He found that disgusting. He offered her Nicola's breakfast orange juice; it was all he had of the soft-drink kind.

'You're having wine, aren't you? I'll have some of that,' she said, evidently not as abstemious as Dermot had been.

Carl handed her a glass of the Pinot Grigio he had bought that afternoon. She took it without a word, then said, 'Haven't you got any nibbles?'

'I'm afraid not.'

'You want to get some in. I shouldn't have them, though. I don't want to put on any more weight.'

Again he felt that thump of the heart. Should he mention the sachets and the leaflet in the hall? Better not. 'Snacks between meals aren't a good idea.' He could hardly believe he had uttered such a sentence. 'Are you on a diet?' was the nearest he would get to touching on the substance and the directions in the hallway.

'I like my food too much for that,' she said. She drank a long draught of her wine. 'Does wine put weight on you?'

'I don't know, Sybil.'

'Give me a fill-up, will you?'

He did, willingly, now that he could sense the question that was coming. 'What's that stuff out in the hallway?'

He wouldn't offer it to her. 'I don't know. Nicola left it there.'

'I'd better go up now. I've got my tea to get.'

Not dinner or supper, but tea. Nicola would call him a snob, and maybe he was. He stood up to see her out, then went back into the room and listened. She had come back down the stairs and was just outside the door. He heard a little sound, a click as of glass tapping on a hard surface, then footsteps on the stairs again.

Waiting for the footfalls to fade up the stairs was the longest he had ever waited for anything in his life, yet it could only have endured for a minute at the most. Then he went outside.

The sachets, leaflet and glass had gone from the table.

CHAPTER THIRTY-TWO

T hat night, Carl made himself scrambled egg on one slice of toast and a can of baked beans on the other. Another bottle of wine remained and a small amount in the bottle he and Sybil had been drinking from. He sat there and listened, though for what he didn't know. A scream? A groan? A stumbling down the stairs? There was silence, a silence that endured for long, slow minutes that seemed like hours. Just before ten, Nicola came home. It occurred to him that he shouldn't have told Sybil that it was Nicola who had put the sachets and the leaflet in the hallway. But surely Sybil wouldn't mention this to Nicola. She never spoke to her. Still, it was a small, niggling worry.

Next day, Sybil went to work, and Carl realised that while he'd been tormenting himself the previous evening, speculating about her brewing up that yellow drink and suffering, perhaps on the verge of death, she had been passing a pleasant few hours.

Her morning departure coincided with Nicola's, and they set off together, sharing an umbrella. They might have been friends, once schoolfellows, chatting away and smiling. Is she telling Nic now? Carl thought. Is she explaining how she took the sachets without permission, just picked them up from the hall table? Why had he been such a fool as to give Sybil that explanation for their presence?

He had still done nothing about a job, so in an effort to put that right and to put Sybil out of his mind, he went into the delicatessen, which was advertising for an assistant. When the manager heard he had no training and no experience, he said he was afraid not. Carl went into the hand car wash, which hadn't advertised, and asked if they wanted anyone. They told him they might in November; men didn't want to work outside in the winter months, so he could come back then. He had plundered Nicola's housekeeping tin so had enough for coffee and even for a very sparse lunch.

Sybil came home at five, which was early for her. Watching her from the ground-floor window, he seemed to see purpose in her heavy tread, as if, on her journey home, she had decided on some particular step to take. She was lost to his sight as she let herself into the house.

Nothing happened. Carl made himself a cup of tea, which if taken without milk was the cheapest thing he could drink. Why had Sybil come home early? Perhaps she'd said she wasn't well. A girl behind the checkout at Lidl couldn't just take a couple of hours off by making an excuse about a delivery or someone reading the meter. But it didn't matter: she was home, and it must be to take the DNP.

It occurred to Carl then how significant DNP had

been in his life, first leading to Dermot's behaviour, his blackmail and his death; now ridding him, he hoped, of Dermot's blackmailing girlfriend. He sat downstairs on Dad's sofa, listening, though for what he didn't know. All he heard was his phone ringing. Nicola.

'A girl I know at work has two tickets for the cinema,' she told him. 'Her friend who was going with her can't, so she's offered it to me. It's for *Before I Go to Sleep*. I won't be late.'

He was glad she wouldn't be there. There might just be silence. On the other hand, there might be shouting or screaming. Sybil might come down complaining of pain or crying. The first symptom would be sweating. Her temperature could go up to 46 degrees. She wouldn't have taken the stuff upstairs with her if she didn't mean at least to try it, he thought. And you couldn't just try DNP; it was all or nothing. He must wait.

Feeling the way he did, tense, slightly sick, screwed up, he couldn't contemplate eating anything. Drink, yes, and there was a whole bottle of wine awaiting him. Screw your courage to the sticking place, he thought, and we'll not fail. That was Macbeth, Macbeth who was going to do murder. Like him. He fetched the wine, opened it, and drank a whole glass straight down.

There was still no sound from upstairs.

Lizzie was sitting outside a restaurant in Clifton Road, reading the *Evening Standard*. Its front page featured what it called the Bus Bomb, and her father's part in it.

239

Like all the other newspapers of the day, the *Standard* was also calling him a hero, the brave man who had carried a ticking bomb off the 55 bus to comparative safety. None of the other papers had mentioned ticking, but all ran the photo of the now famous Thomas Milsom, described (inaccurately) as a press photographer. The 'happily married bus rider' and his 'beautiful daughter Elizabeth' lived (again inaccurately) in a 'fine detached home' in north-west London. Mr Milsom, known to his many friends as Tom, would certainly receive an award for bravery, and possibly an OBE from the Queen. On an inside page was another photo of Tom, with Lizzie and Dot this time, and a picture of the roadway where the bomb had gone off and of the injured being taken away on stretchers.

Feeling pleased for her dad, and even more pleased with her own coverage, Lizzie drank her coffee and ate the chocolate biscuit that came with it. She picked up the large plastic carrier containing the late Dermot McKinnon's property and hoisted its straps on to her shoulder. It was ten to seven. Leaving the *Evening Standard* on the table, she went inside to pay.

The girl behind the till also had a *Standard*, and did a double take. 'That's you! That's your dad! You must be so proud of him.'

It felt to Lizzie quite a long walk to Falcon Mews, especially as she was carrying a heavy bag and wearing high heels. Adam phoned when she was in Castellain

Road. He'd finished the work he was doing and said he would come and meet her. 'Amazing about your dad. It's been all over the papers. There's a picture of you, too.'

Lizzie said she'd seen it, and told him the number of the mews house where she'd be.

Five minutes later, she was ringing the doorbell.

Carl put the television on and caught the bus bomb story. He seemed to remember that man Milsom from years ago; he'd been at school with his daughter, he thought. Impossible to concentrate, though. He switched it off and went back to where he had been sitting for the past half-hour, almost at the top of the upper flight of stairs, as near as he could to the top flat. And he had been rewarded by sounds. Not very loud sounds; in fact sounds that could hardly be identified, grunts really, and sighs, nothing more than that. He noticed that Sybil's front door was slightly open.

The doorbell ringing shocked him; it made him furiously angry. It seldom happened, and when it did, it was like an insult, an intrusion and an assault. Who dared come here, and *now*? It rang again.

He ran downstairs to answer it. He needed to get rid of whoever it was. He opened the door, flinging it back.

'Yes? What is it?'

A girl stood outside, a girl who seemed vaguely familiar. 'Hi, Carl. Long time no see,' she said. 'I've brought some stuff from the pet clinic that belonged to Dermot McKinnon. I believe he lived in the top flat? We didn't know where else to take it.' She stepped in, swinging a large bag, before he could stop her

'You can't go up!' he shouted.

But she was already on the stairs, and he could only have stopped her now by seizing hold of her. A shrill cry came from behind the half-open door on the top floor, followed by a hoarse sobbing.

Lizzie ran up another four or five steps, stopped and called, 'What's that? What's going on up there?'

'Not your business,' Carl said, adding, absurdly, 'You're trespassing!'

Lizzie dropped the bag and flung open the door. A girl of about her own age was rolling on the floor, sweating so much that her face and arms looked as if they'd been dipped in water. Vomit splashed the rug and soaked the armchair she had tumbled out of.

A quick memory of how she had failed to do anything when she was herself threatened came back to Lizzie. She hesitated no longer but took her mobile out of her coat pocket and dialled the emergency number. 'Ambulance,' she shouted. 'Eleven Falcon Mews, West Nine.'

She thought of Carl, how they'd been to school together and that he'd been a friend of Stacey. He didn't seem to recognise her, and she wasn't going to remind him, especially not now.

He had disappeared downstairs, and a good thing too. She knelt down beside the girl and told her it was all right, help was coming. They'd take her to hospital, St Mary's probably.

'What's your name?'

'Sybil.' It came out as a choked whisper.

'I can hear the ambulance now.'

I've learned from what happened with Scotty and Redhead, Lizzie thought. Once I'd have been in a real panic, but not now. I'm stronger now.

'Don't leave me,' sobbed Sybil.

'I have to let them in, but I'll be right back.'

Running down the stairs, Lizzie flung open the front door as the ambulance came howling round the mews. A man and a woman jumped out, and ran across the cobbles carrying what looked like a stretcher.

'Upstairs!' cried Lizzie.

She went into the living room, where Carl lay face-downwards on a sofa. In the kitchen she poured a glass of water and drank it down. 'What did you do to her, you bastard?' she said as she passed him on her way back. Upstairs, the paramedics had laid Sybil on the stretcher and were covering her with a white blanket.

'You'll be OK now,' Lizzie said. 'You're safe.'

She went back downstairs, and out through the front door. Carl needed to stop her, explain. But Adam was coming along the mews, and when he saw her, he put out his arms. Lizzie went into them and he hugged her tightly.

'Can we get away from here?' she said. 'I really don't want to stay here a moment longer. It brings back too many memories of something bad that happened to me. I'll explain. It's time I explained.'

They held hands down Castellain Road. 'Oh dear,' she

said after a while, 'I haven't a clue what I did with Dermot's stuff. I must have dropped it.'

'I'm sure it doesn't matter at all,' said Adam. 'It's just so great to be walking down the street with you.'

T he battery of Carl's mobile phone appeared to have gone flat. Nicola tried the landline, but no one answered. Leaving a message when all you wanted to say was that you hadn't liked the film and left early was pointless. The ambulance that passed her bus on the way home she didn't connect with Falcon Mews. Why should she? By now it was growing dark, but there were no lights on in number 11. On the front path someone had dropped a crumpled tissue, and further along a ballpoint pen. The front door had been left on the latch. Balancing her shopping, she pushed it open, went in and called, 'Carl?'

No answer. He wasn't in the living room or the kitchen or upstairs, and the front door of Sybil's flat stood wide open. Indoors it seemed stuffy and close, oppressive. Feeling deeply uneasy, Nicola put the hallway light on, opened the front door and stood on the step. Light poured out, filling the little front garden. Mr Kaleejah and Elinor Jackson from next door came out simultaneously to ask if anything was wrong.

'I see the ambulance,' said Mr Kaleejah, 'and I think someone is taken ill, someone has an accident.'

Elinor's partner came out to join her. They suggested Nicola come into their house, offered a drink. Had she called the police? Nicola said no to everything, thanks but no. She had to be indoors, she said, in case the phone rang. Mr Kaleejah's dog threw back its head and started howling, not a bark but a wolf-like howl.

Back inside, Nicola put a light on in the living room and saw something move in a dark corner. She nearly screamed but controlled herself by clasping her hand over her mouth. She sat down on 'Dad's sofa', got up again, said, 'What are you doing?' and then, when there was no answer, 'What's going on?'

'Why have you come here?' he said.

'Carl? Tell me what's going on. There was an ambulance. What's happened?'

He was silent for so long she thought he wasn't going to speak to her. Then at last he said in a voice she barely recognised, 'Sybil. They took her away.'

'What's happened to her?'

She was looking at a man she wouldn't have recognised but for his voice. She thought of people she'd read about whose hair turned white overnight from shock. That could happen to Carl; it looked as if it would, though she had never really believed it possible.

'You must sit down,' he said. 'And I will tell you. She took poison. Someone came to the house and found her and called an ambulance.'

'What do you mean?'

'I've been in her flat. There's sick all over the place. She nearly died; she probably is dead now.'

'What poison?' said Nicola in a voice that didn't sound like her own.

'I don't know. It doesn't matter.'

'I am going to look.'

'No, don't. Don't. It's not your business.'

But she was on the stairs. He followed her, clambering up, too weak to do anything but crawl. The big room where Sybil had sweated and struggled stank of vomit. Carl crept across the floor on all fours, making whimpering sounds. It was clear to him that the paramedics must have taken away with them the sachets that had contained the DNP.

Nicola covered her nose with a handful of tissues from her bag. 'It was that same stuff you sold to Stacey, wasn't it?'

'She got it herself online,' he muttered.

'No. No, Carl. You gave it to her. I saw it in our bathroom, a powder in sachets it was. I don't suppose you sold it this time. Let's go downstairs. I can't stand this smell.' At the foot, she sat on the bottom stair. 'Whatever she held over you, whatever Dermot did, I don't want to know. I'm frightened of you, Carl.'

He went past her and stood holding on to the table. He noticed how she flinched. 'There's nothing to be frightened of. I'll tell you everything. I won't keep anything back.'

'You've killed her, haven't you? I never thought I would say that to anyone. It's the most terrible thing anyone can say.' Nicola got up and pulled her coat round her as if she was cold. Her face was white and her hands shook. 'I can't stay here with you.'

'Don't leave me,' he said. 'Please don't leave me.'

He took hold of her by the shoulders and pulled her to him. Any other girl, he thought later, would have kicked out at him, fought him. Nicola let herself go limp in his arms, then gently slipped out of them, putting out her hand to open the front door. He stepped back in a kind of shame.

'Let me go, Carl,' she said in her clear, resounding voice. 'Let me go.'

She stepped out into the dark. It had rained since she came back, and the darkness was shiny with yellow light on wet cobbles and silvery slates.

He ran after her, calling to her to come back. But when she turned the corner into Castellain Road, he gave up. Moaning softly, whimpering, he sat down on a front step and put his head in his hands.

CHAPTER THIRTY-FOUR

He lay awake for hours, aware that things always appeared so much worse at night. The knowledge that these fears and horrors would surely shrink away in the morning, assuming their natural size, did nothing to calm him. He tossed and turned, thinking of Sybil dead in a mortuary somewhere and, uselessly, pointlessly, of the mess and filth upstairs, the room that smelt so bad that Nicola had had to leave it behind and run away. At about three, before it began to get light, he fell asleep, and went on sleeping until sunshine streaming in woke him up.

It was only then that the horrid sequence of events came back to him, gradually, one at a time, until he was overwhelmed by fear and a physical pain that squeezed his stomach like a griping indigestion and doubled him up. He was frightened to lie there, twisted up, and forced himself out on to the floor, a severely painful cramp in both legs. The sound he heard he couldn't identify; it seemed to him the strangest sound he had ever heard, until at last he recognised it as the phone, the landline.

He let it ring until it seemed to get tired and stopped. The ensuing silence was so beautiful – he told himself it was beautiful – that he thought if losing his hearing would bring this blissful nothingness, he would welcome deafness.

In the sweet quiet he got on to all fours, then hoisted himself to his feet. It took a little while. He made his way very slowly into the kitchen. The first thing he saw was the shopping bag Nicola had brought in with her the previous evening. Inside were apples, a cut loaf, sliced cheese, a half-litre of milk, two tins of sardines and six large eggs. He pulled out the crust end of the loaf, laid a slice of Cheddar on it and sat on a stool to eat. He ripped the top off the milk container and took a deep swig, the first milk, he thought, he had drunk since he was a child. It was ten past eleven. Now that he was fully awake, he felt much better and stronger. The woman was dead. She had killed herself just as Stacey had killed herself, from vanity, from a willingness to do anything fast and easy to achieve weight loss, even if that anything was suicidal. Of course she hadn't known that, the poor foolish creature; she hadn't been the sort of woman who read labels with cautionary advice on them.

He knew he must, at any rate superficially, clean up that top flat, and went upstairs carrying a bucket with him. The smell in the room wasn't nearly as bad as Nicola had said. A slightly sour whiff, that was all. He filled the bucket with hot soapy water from the kitchen, and scraped the vomit off the rugs and cushions before deciding to put the cushions in a plastic bag and then in the rubbish bin by the back gate. The stains left behind on the various textiles he scrubbed with a brush he found under the sink. It wasn't all that long a job once he got down to it, and by midday the task was completed. It was only then, when evidence of what had happened had been removed, that he realised what Sybil's death meant: that the life of the second unwelcome occupant of the top flat at 11 Falcon Mews was over.

'It seems to be a fine day,' he said aloud. 'I shall make myself some lunch – two eggs, I think, and a piece of toast – and then I'll go out and walk up to my mother's. I'll borrow enough money from her to tide me over until I can get a tenant set up in the top flat. It shouldn't take long.'

He broke the two eggs into a bowl, beat them with a fork, scrambled the mixture in a saucepan and made the toast. His lunch was almost eaten when the doorbell rang. It made him jump. He told himself not to be stupid, that there was no need to answer it. But when the bell rang again, he went to the door.

Sybil's father stood outside. He was carrying a suitcase. No doubt he had come to tell Carl what he already knew: that Sybil was dead.

'You'd better come in,' Carl said.

'I won't stop,' Cliff Soames said. 'Sybil's back with us now. The hospital sent her home this morning. I've come for her things.'

Was this how it felt when you knew you were going

to faint? Carl clutched hold of the table top. Cliff came in, slamming the door behind him.

'They got most of that stuff out of her. They said she'll be OK now, but she'll not be coming back here. Not ever. Her mum's looking after her, won't let her out of her sight. She won't think of leaving us again. I'll go up and put her things in the case.'

Carl went into the living room and sat on Dad's sofa as Cliff Soames's words sank in. Sybil wasn't coming back here, Sybil wasn't dead; they didn't all die, the people who took DNP, not the ones who were careful. He began to shake, his hands trembling, the muscles in his legs jumping. The suitcase Cliff had brought, now full, bumped down the stairs. He left it in the hall, took a step into the room.

'Sybil wants to stay alive,' he said, his tone ominous. 'You'll never set eyes on her again. Does she owe you any rent?'

Carl didn't know what to say. The real sum she owed he was afraid to put into words, but the temptation to say something, to name a small figure, was too great to resist.

'Eighty pounds,' he said, and stupidly, 'If you can see your way . . .'

Cliff Soames pulled a wad of notes out of his pocket, handed them over and said he'd like a receipt. 'The rents you people charge. I've read about you in the papers, greedy, grasping buggers. I hope it chokes you.'

Carl wrote a receipt for eighty pounds and handed it over in silence. When the front door slammed, he watched Cliff stagger down the street with the heavy bag. His first task, he thought, would be to spend some of the money he was still clutching on a couple of bottles of wine, and perhaps a bottle of something stronger.

I t was Saturday, it had to be. Carl's priority was to look at accommodation wanted online and pick one or two people who seemed likely. But there were hundreds of them – probably thousands – all wanting somewhere to live in central London. Investigating these things really brought it home to you how desperate the housing situation was.

He soon saw that the place he had to offer, a self-contained top floor of a mews house in Maida Vale, was about as desirable as you could get, and the rent he had asked (though scarcely ever succeeded in getting) had been derisory. This would have to be revised. Within ten minutes he had increased it considerably and had arranged for three applicants to come round later: a couple at two, a single man at four and a woman at six. What to do if he really liked the first one he didn't yet know. He would give it some thought.

After a shot of vodka and a glass of Pinot Grigio, he began looking through his part of the house for Nicola's property. She must have left a lot of things behind, he thought: clothes, maybe jewellery, though she hadn't much, make-up and perfume (to which the same applied), books, CDs and DVDs. But she hadn't; just a bit of underwear, and a grey dress and a red dress for work, and jeans and sweaters or T-shirts for the weekends. The grey dress was still in the wardrobe and so was a pair of jeans and a blue and white patterned top he had always liked. It gave him a pang to look at it; it was as if she had died.

The doorbell rang while he was wondering what to do next. It was Mr and Mrs Crowhurst, right on time. They looked very young, about his own age or younger. The rent he was asking – the new rent – seemed not to put them off. They walked around the rooms, Mrs Crowhurst sniffing the air in the living room rather suspiciously but making no comment. Could they use the garden? Carl remembered last time and said no, he was afraid not. Mr Crowhurst said they were called Jason and Chloe but had said they were Mr and Mrs because married people sounded more respectable.

'Aren't you married, then?'

'Oh yes, we're married all right.' They held out their left hands to show their wedding rings. 'We'll call you and let you know.'

'I've got two more people coming, one at four and one at six, so don't be too long about it.' Carl had never felt so powerful, monarch of all he surveyed, as Dermot might have said.

The next possible tenant came at ten past four. He was old enough to be the Crowhursts' father, tall, grey-haired, wearing a suit. His name was Andrew Page, and whether he was married didn't come into it. He agreed to the rent, didn't ask about the use of the garden but said he would like to move in as soon as possible. There was something about him that reminded Carl of Dermot. He said he had one more applicant to see, and Mr Page was to call later.

When the phone rang at five, Carl thought it must be Andrew Page, but it was a man called Harry who said he was a friend of Nicola's and would like to come round in his jalopy and pick up her stuff. Now, if poss. Carl said the following day would be more convenient, but that didn't suit Harry.

'It must be now or never,' said Harry.

Harry seemed unlike any possible friend of Nicola's. He wore a paint-stained tracksuit and had a big bushy beard as well as shoulder-length hair. It was as well, Carl thought, that Nicola wasn't clothes-conscious, for Harry had brought only two large whitish pillow cases to put everything in. This was a task he accomplished in about five minutes, before hurling the pillow cases into the back of the van and driving off much faster, Carl thought, than anyone had ever before sped along the cobbles. He had tried to persuade Harry to take Nicola's green goose with him, but Harry had looked at it and shook his head. So there it sat on the hall table, a silent and reproachful reminder of everything that had happened to Carl over the past few months.

Immediately after the van departed, a small woman who introduced herself as Mrs Hamilton drove up in a silver Lexus. Before she had even entered the house she was back in the car and driving away, once Carl had told her there was no off-street parking available at 11 Falcon Mews.

Andrew Page returned in a taxi just before eight. 'Turned up like a bad penny,' he said, which was so like Dermot that it made Carl shudder.

'Changed your mind, have you?' Carl said, almost hoping that he had. But Andrew Page hadn't. He simply wanted to know that nothing had happened to keep him from the tenancy. Nothing had, Carl said rather reluctantly.

'I'd like to come back tomorrow with my solicitor to sign the contract. Oh, and pay the deposit. Best to have things all open and above board, don't you think?'

Carl had never heard of anyone having a solicitor present for such a transaction, but he didn't know much about letting property. He had certainly made a mess of it last time. It seemed amazing to him too that this man wanted to give him a deposit without even being asked for it. While the taxi waited, they arranged for him to return at six p.m. the following day with Mr Lucas Partridge, LLB.

Throughout the rest of the evening, Carl repeated to himself the two clichés Andrew Page had uttered, Dermot-like. What did it matter? He intended to avoid speaking to him as much as possible during his tenancy. The money was good and would keep on coming – without hindrance, without blackmail.

'What would you do,' said Adam, 'if you recognised someone you'd seen doing something weird and you thought he might have committed a crime?'

He and Lizzie were walking along the canal towpath between Cunningham Place and Lisson Green. It was a fine, clear evening. 'What d'you mean by weird?' said Lizzie.

'Sit down a minute.'

They sat on a seat on the bank. 'The guy who used to do your job at the pet place – what was he called?'

'Dermot McKinnon. He was murdered.'

'I know he was,' said Adam. 'It happened in a street called Jerome something. Jerome Crescent, I think. They never found who did it.' He paused. 'At approximately that time, I'm not exactly sure of the date, I was on my way to drinks with a friend at a pub in Camden, and was cycling along the path where we are now and under the bridge on Park Road until I was on the edge of the park, and this guy was on the opposite bank with a big backpack. It was getting dark and he didn't see me.'

'What guy, Adam?'

'The man whose house you took McKinnon's stuff to. He was standing at the door when I met you in the street that day. He's the man I saw with the backpack. I watched him from the bank through the trees. I know he didn't see me. I was fascinated. He squatted down, undid the bag and took a big heavy thing out of it. Then I saw him throw the bag into the canal, but not the heavy object, which he sort of cradled in his arms. It was all very odd.'

'Oh my God,' said Lizzie.

'I hadn't given it much thought until recently. At the time, I didn't know who he was, certainly didn't know there was any connection between him and the man

257

who was murdered. So it gave me quite a shock to recognise him.'

'Carl Martin?'

'Yes. And he and Dermot McKinnon lived in the same house. It's an odd coincidence, don't you think?'

The deposit, refundable on the termination of the tenancy, was so welcome to Carl, and so unexpected, he could scarcely believe it even when the cheque for two thousand pounds was put into his hand. Mr Partridge, the solicitor, seemed to find nothing strange in this transaction. That Carl had prepared no contract between landlord and tenant caused some shaking of his head, but no great harm was done as on Page's instructions he had created one himself. All of it looked very favourable to Carl, another cause of wonderment, so that he felt he must be living in a happy dream. He half expected to wake up and find himself back in the real world without money, food or any sort of security.

The contract was signed and witnessed. If it was agreeable to Mr Martin, as his new tenant insisted on calling him, Andrew Page would move in the next day. He would bring some small items of furniture, if that was all right with Mr Martin. Carl, still dazed from the windfall and promises of further cash, said it was fine. When the two men had gone, he looked hard at the cheque. It really was for two thousand pounds. It was funny that he now had all this money but not a single note or coin, and wouldn't have until he cashed the cheque in the morning.

He would have liked to celebrate by going to the Summerhouse restaurant nearby, or the newly opened Crocker's Folly, and treating himself to oysters and steak and a bottle of champagne. Then he remembered his credit card, which hadn't been used for months – he hadn't dared to use it; he now couldn't recall where he had put it. It took him half an hour before he located it in the pocket of a jacket he never wore.

It was dinner time, precisely seven thirty. He strolled along Sutherland Avenue and across the Edgware Road into Aberdeen Place. Crocker's Folly was grand outside, and its greatly refurbished interior very pretty and elegant. They had no oysters, but steak and champagne were no problem. It was so long since Carl had drunk champagne that he had forgotten what it tasted like. He wasn't going to gobble his food, but ate it in a leisurely fashion, sipping the champagne and savouring the sautéed potatoes. He had moved from this delicious first course on to a confection of three kinds of chocolate and Cornish ice cream before allowing himself to think about his life and what was happening to it.

Maybe Nicola would come back now that he had a new tenant and money, though money had never attracted her. He could see his friends again, phone them, visit them and ask them over. He would resume the abandoned novel; he would find that writing afforded him the pleasure it once had, he would find inspiration. His worries were all past and he must take care not to create new ones by getting on overly friendly terms with Andrew Page. Perhaps 'Mr Martin' and 'Mr Page' was the best policy, so there would be no need for invitations to drinks or even cups of tea.

He had begun the walk back to Falcon Mews when thoughts of Dermot McKinnon came into his mind. Surely now that his new life was taking shape, the memory of Dermot would fade. There could be no pity, no regret. What he had done had been very close to an accident, in that he had hardly known what was happening until it was all over. In a year's time, after a year of enjoying the new tenant, with his formal ways and cold correctness, he would have ceased altogether to remember Dermot, and certainly wouldn't blame himself in any way for his death.

'Are you going to do anything about it?'

'I don't know,' Adam said. He and Lizzie were alone in the reception area of the Sutherland Pet Clinic. The clinic was closed, but one patient, a King Charles spaniel, and its owner remained. They were in Caroline's examination room, where the dog, Louis Quatorze, was receiving immunisation. 'I could go to the police, I know that. I would tell them what I've told you: that at what I think was roughly the time of the murder, I believe I saw Carl Martin holding the instrument he'd used to kill Dermot McKinnon.'

'Are you going to go to the police?'

Adam sighed. 'I saw a man drop something into the canal where it goes into Regent's Park. I didn't come forward earlier because I didn't think any more of it till I went to pick you up in Falcon Mews and that same man – no doubt about that – came out of the house on to the front steps. You told me that Dermot McKinnon had also lived there, in the top flat. It doesn't amount to much, does it?'

Before she could reply, Caroline emerged with Louis Quatorze and his owner. Lizzie presented the owner with her bill and patted Louis on the head. She and Adam left at the same time as the dog and his owner, leaving Caroline to lock up.

'Do you really think he might have killed Dermot?' Lizzie said. She remembered the callous way Carl had behaved when Sybil had been so ill upstairs. But still, could he have committed murder?

'I don't know, Lizzie. Let's go to the Prince Alfred pub and have a drink. It's too cold to be outside.'

In the pub, Lizzie sat at one of the little tables and Adam fetched two glasses of white wine. 'What I'd like would be to talk to Carl about it,' he said. 'Find out how he reacts. I'd like to know his state of mind.'

'Well, you are training to be a psychologist,' said Lizzie.

Adam laughed. 'I've got a psychology degree, but that's about it. You know, I'd just like to see him. I think I'd tell him I don't intend to go to the police, but when I've heard him out – if he consents to speak to me – I'll tell him he should go to them himself.'

'What – and confess?'

'That would be the general idea.'

'But people don't do that, Adam. Not voluntarily. And what happens if he gets violent? If you're right and he did kill Dermot, what's to stop him killing again?'

The previous winter had not been cold. It had been wet instead, and if you lived near the Thames or in the Somerset Levels you stood a serious chance of being flooded. This year the warm weather had gone on and on, but as autumn turned into winter, sharp cold began. London was always the mildest part of the United Kingdom, and the cold started in Maida Vale rather later than elsewhere. But by the end of November in Falcon Mews, frost was glittering on the bushes that lined the cobbled street, and silvering the bare branches of the trees.

In number 11, the central heating, which hadn't been put to the test the previous year, was soon needed and found wanting. At least in Carl's opinion. At the top of the house, in the tenant's domain, there were no complaints, but one evening Carl happened to be in the hall when Andrew Page came in with two large electric heaters he fetched from the back of a taxi.

'I'm a bit of a chilly mortal,' he said by way of explanation. 'I'm sure the heating's adequate.'

The heaters were taken upstairs and, as always, Andrew Page's front door was closed silently. Carl's only way of knowing if his tenant was in was to go out into the street or the back garden and look up to see if a light was on behind the top windows. Even that was hardly a sure guide, as people all too often went out leaving lights on, and Andrew Page might be one of them. But Carl had no desire to know. Everyone had television, so presumably Andrew had. Most had a radio or music player or both, so no doubt he had one of those too. But if he did, no sound was ever heard from the top-floor rooms. No running water, nothing dropped on the floor, no click of a switch, no phone ringing, no computer coming on. Andrew Page seemed to live in utter silence. In that respect, in *all* respects, he was the ideal tenant. The rent was received without fail in Carl's bank account on the last day of every month. Carl sometimes thought Andrew Page was too good to be true, but he told himself that he felt that way because until very recently the people he had come across had been – not to put too fine a point on it – degenerate bastards.

All was well in Carl's life, except for the loss of Nicola. He'd discovered that she no longer lived in Ashmill Street, which meant that she had got herself other accommodation, and he could only find out where this was by calling her office at the Department of Health. In other words by calling her, and he shied away from doing that. He had to face it. If she wanted to see him, to be with him again, she would phone him. He remembered their parting, and that man coming round in his 'jalopy' to collect her things. Walking past a mirror, the only one in the house outside the bathroom, he stopped and made himself smile into it. As he feared, his smile had become a facial distortion, like a mask or a gargoyle, with no warmth or friendliness in it.

In the mornings and sometimes in the evenings he worked on his novel, mechanically, almost automatically, typing words that all meant something, describing events or people or actions. Remembering Raymond Chandler's advice to authors that, when at a loss, they should have a man come into a room with a gun, Carl introduced scenes of violence in order to liven up his story. Then, when he had almost decided to abandon the novel and accept that he was to be a one-book author, Andrew Page came down the stairs and, instead of leaving the house, tapped on his living room door.

Carl had been sitting at the laptop, his hands idle, staring at the blank screen with its green hill far away. He called out to come in, and Andrew entered the room holding a copy of *Death's Door*.

'Sorry to disturb you,' he said, 'but I was hoping you'd sign this. I bought it this afternoon in that little bookshop round the corner.'

Only Carl's publisher and a friend of his publisher had ever put this request to him before.

'Of course I will.' Carl wondered if the smile with which he agreed looked as sinister and forced as the toothy grimace he had an hour before achieved in the mirror. If it did, it had no adverse effect on Andrew Page, who handed over the book open at the title page and Carl signed it. Some instinct from the past must have inspired him, for, repeating the grim smile, he asked his tenant to stay for a while and have a drink. These days the flat was always well stocked with wine and spirits.

'Thanks. I'd like to.'

Carl produced gin and a bottle of tonic, white wine and a couple of cans of lager, all of it suitably chilled. He was already regretting his offer, not because he cared how much Andrew Page consumed, but for want of knowing what to talk about. In fact it was easy, because the hitherto silent Andrew did most of the talking. He turned out to be a trainee solicitor with a law degree, soon approaching the end of his two-year articles. This, Carl thought, probably accounted for him bringing a solicitor along with him for the signing and witnessing of the contract. Andrew Page explained that both his mother and father were solicitors and his older brother was a barrister. He moved on to say how lucky he was to have found this flat in this nice street and how much he liked living here. He was engaged and intended to marry as soon as he qualified. He seemed to believe that Carl was a successful author with several best-selling books behind him, and Carl was on the point of denying this when the phone rang.

It was a man called Adam Yates that Carl had never heard of. He had a nice voice, civilised and educated, which meant nothing. 'You know my girlfriend, Lizzie Milsom.'

Did he? The name seemed familiar. A school friend,

he thought. Back when he and Stacey were children. All so long ago.

'I won't keep you,' said Adam Yates. 'I just want to talk with you for a few minutes. I could come round about eight.'

Could he put it off till tomorrow? Carl wondered. But if he did, he would worry all night and half the next day. He suggested nine.

Adam Yates said nine would be fine. Carl put the phone down and apologised to Andrew Page. They talked a little longer. His guest refused another drink but as he was leaving said, 'If I can be of any assistance, please feel free to ask me. I've been thinking for a long time now that you might need help.' He let himself out, closing the door behind him. Carl felt rather humiliated. And worried. Had his troubles, or the memory of them, shown so plainly, and not just in his rictus smile?

He had two hours to wait for Adam Yates, whoever he was. A friend of Lizzie Milsom's, he had said. Adam Yates would come and talk to him about whatever it was. But the phone call had transported him back to the foodless life of the previous summer, the time when more and more drink was needed and eating was impossible. He wanted nothing to eat now, but to drink another glass of wine would be stupid, especially considering the three he had already had with Andrew. He needed to be able to defend himself.

Defend? There was nothing this man could accuse him of or suggest he had done wrong; nothing, surely, that would call forth a defence.

At ten to nine, Carl went upstairs and stationed himself at the window that looked on to the mews. Would Adam Yates come in a car? Or by taxi? If he was a Londoner, he would more likely arrive on foot. He sat in darkness and watched by the light of the street lamp that was outside Mr Kaleejah's. The mews was deserted, lights on in most of the houses. It was a fine night, the moon not yet risen but a single star showing, bright and steady. The Pole Star? Carl kept his eyes on his watch. At one minute to nine, Mr Kaleejah came out of his front door with his dog on a lead and its rubber bone in its mouth. Slowly and purposely they set off in the Castellain Road direction. On the dot of nine, a man of about Carl's own age appeared at the other end of the mews. Carl went downstairs to answer the door, feeling sick for the first time in months. He was back in that state he recognised of perpetual anxiety.

He opened the door and the man he had seen from the window said, 'Adam Yates.'

Carl nodded. He stepped back and Adam Yates came in. He was a little taller than Carl, his dark hair cut short, clean-shaven so closely as somehow to have an official look. To Carl, his appearance and his neat jacket and matching trousers suggested a detective inspector in a TV serial. He followed Carl into the living room and was offered a drink.

'This isn't a social call,' Adam said. 'It won't take long.'

Carl, retreating into his old world of fear and dread, was longing for a drink. Two bottles of wine, one white and the other rosé, stood on the table by Dad's sofa. His craving was strong, but not strong enough to break through the inhibition that competed with it. He told Adam to sit down and sat down himself on the sofa, as if the proximity of the bottles could be a comfort. In fact the reverse was true.

'What do you want to say to me?'

'The event that I want to talk about happened last September,' said Adam. 'By the canal.'

I knew it, Carl thought. Another blackmailer. How could he have believed he was safe, that everything was all right, that there was nothing more to fear? He nodded, moving his head slowly, said, 'Can I have a drink?'

'If you need it. I see you do.'

Carl filled a glass from the Sauvignon bottle. The wine had grown warm, but that was unimportant. It had never been so much needed or tasted so good.

'I was on the canal bank, up among the trees,' Adam Yates said. 'I saw you come along the bank below me, kneel down and take a heavy object out of your backpack which you then dropped into the canal. Of course I wondered why, but I didn't put it together with the murder of Dermot McKinnon. I didn't even hear about the murder until some time later. I didn't know you had any connection to Dermot until I came to Falcon Mews to meet Lizzie and I saw you come out of your front door.'

Carl said nothing. There was no point. This man, who looked like a detective but obviously wasn't, knew everything. He swallowed half the contents of the wine glass.

'I wanted to tell you that I know what you've done,' Adam said.

Carl sat back, his mind clear suddenly. 'Well, don't think you're alone,' he said. 'Dermot McKinnon knew about the first girl who died, and blackmailed me by withholding the rent. After he was dead, his girlfriend came to live here and blackmailed me again by with-holding the rent. You can't aim to do that because you don't pay me rent.'

Adam seemed surprised by this. 'You've had a bad time,' he said reasonably.

'Worse even than all this: my girlfriend guessed what had happened and left me. I've got a good tenant for the top flat now, but maybe he'll leave when you tell your story, because I'm not paying you blackmail money. I've had enough of that. I'm not paying you to keep silent. I'm not handing over to you the rent my tenant pays or letting you live in part of the house rent-free.'

'I'm not asking you to let me live in your house,' said Adam. 'I haven't asked for anything.' He refilled Carl's glass. 'I don't even want wine from you.'

This made Carl wince. The man was so calm. So quietly condemning. 'What's the point of all this then?'

'I just wanted you to know that I know,' Adam said. He leaned forward, his voice still reasonable, soothing even. 'What I'd really like is for you to go to the police and confess what you did. You'd not have any worries then. It would all be over. You'd go to prison, but confessing would shorten your sentence.'

For a moment Carl felt an immense burden lift from his shoulders as he considered a life free from anxiety and fear. But then reality came crashing back. 'Why should I?' he said. 'I've got a peaceful life now. I've enough to live on, everything's worked out for me. Why the hell should I confess?'

'Because I know,' Adam said. 'And you know that I know. Look, I'm not interested in retribution or punishment. I promise you I will never tell a soul, and I keep my promises. But why would you believe me? In fact, I can see right now by the look on your face that you don't.'

He got up. 'I'll give your kind regards to Lizzie, shall I? She says you were at school together, but I'm sure you remembered that when she came round with Dermot's things.' He turned and looked at Carl. 'I can see you're suffering, but there is a way to end this, and you know what that is.'

Of course he didn't believe what Adam Yates had said. You don't believe someone who makes a promise and then says he doesn't break them. Anyone can say that. After sleeping well for weeks, Carl lay awake that night. He thought of everything Adam had said, repeated it over and over, considered the man's promise and dismissed it. He would tell. The police would put it all together. It was only a matter of time.

But the weeks went by, and then months. Andrew Page continued to pay the rent on the last day of each month. Mr Kaleejah continued to take his dog out three or four times a day, and Carl's neighbours said good morning and hi and how are you when they encountered him.

One fine day Nicola came round. By that time he was drinking again, and as heavily as he had done in the days after Sybil had returned to her parents. Nicola refused a drink but asked if she could make herself a cup of tea. She made the tea and produced the white chocolate biscuits he had always liked but hadn't eaten since she had left him. She told him she had met someone else, was living with him. They were getting married soon. Nothing of course was said about Dermot or Sybil or Stacey, and nothing about money. Nicola left after half an hour.

Carl watched her from the window, keeping his eyes on her until she had turned out of the mews into Sutherland Avenue. All the time she was with him, he had been drinking, no longer bothering to hide his habit from visitors and friends. Of all of them, only his mother reproached him for drinking so much. Nicola had said nothing. From her face, he thought he could see that she no longer cared.

Now that she was gone, he opened his third bottle of wine of the day and poured himself a large glass. The stronger kinds of alcohol, the whisky and gin and vodka, sent him to sleep quite quickly, but wine only made him feel rather dazed; as if nothing mattered very much. It took away for a time the damning sentences that kept repeating in his head: *You murdered Dermot, you killed him*, and Adam Yates's *There is a way to end this, and you know what that is*. The words combined to make a kind of mantra.

Nearly a year had passed since Dermot's death, six months since Adam Yates had come to tell him what he knew. He kept up his habit of walking, and now roamed further and over larger areas, covering Regent's Park and exploring Primrose Hill. Breakfast started with a large glass of wine, a tumbler not a wine glass, which was refilled, so that when he began on his walk, he was dizzy with drink and had to sit down on a roadside seat, sometimes to fall asleep. He had ceased to write anything. The few attempts he had made to start something new he gave up after a paragraph or two. The rent continued to come in, though, and even after he had settled his utilities bills and the council tax and his small amount of income tax, the money mounted up.

Still, he bought the cheapest wine because there was no point in buying the expensive stuff. He drank it without tasting it, swallowing it fast to bring a few hours' oblivion, and grew even thinner. His mother, whom he occasionally saw because, despairing of his visiting her, she came to visit him, told him that he looked more like his father than ever. For the first time in months he looked in the mirror, and saw a skeletal man with staring eyes and protruding bones.

Increasingly now his thoughts were centred not on Dermot's murder but on Adam Yates's knowledge of it. Few people visited him, and those who did were postmen or someone come to read a meter. He fancied that they stared at the scanty beard he had grown, and his emaciated body.

For a long time after Adam's visit, Carl was sure that every ring on the doorbell must be the police. Of course Adam would have reported him, he told himself. Of course he would; his promise meant nothing.

He spent whole days thinking of nothing but Adam, about what he'd said, and the soothing tone of his voice when he'd told him that his worries could soon be over. He thought too of what must happen next, of the step that must be taken to restore the peace of mind he'd had before he crashed the green goose down on Dermot's head. He had dreams about that earlier time, and although he knew he had been in a perpetual state of anxiety and bitter regret, he looked back on it now as calm and carefree.

Adam Yates had been right: if he wanted that peaceful life back again, there was only one way to do it.

'He's a very serious young man,' said Dot Milsom. 'He acts more like a man twice his age.'

'Who does?' Tom asked.

'Lizzie's young man, Adam.'

'He's a cut above any boyfriend she's ever had.' Tom looked up from his newspaper. 'And very clever. Quite nice too, don't you think? At least he's got some manners.'

Tom, who had given up his joyriding on buses – as Dot called it – in favour of a modified form of motorbike tracking on a ploughed field, turned to the crime pages and gave a low whistle.

'What is it, Tom?'

'Wasn't Lizzie at school with a boy called Carl Martin?'

Dot nodded. 'What's he done?'

'He appears to have confessed to murder,' Tom said. 'Remember that chap who was hit over the head in Jerome Crescent? Well, that was Carl. Who did it, I mean. It says here that he walked into a police station and confessed. Imagine doing that!'

'I'd be too scared,' said Dot.

Tom shook his head, more in sorrow than anger. 'It

wouldn't be as scary as not confessing,' he said. 'It might even be a comfort. Think what it must have been like to have that on his conscience.'

He put his newspaper down and leaned back in his chair. 'And now,' he said, 'now it's all over.'